THE CONTRIVED GODDESS

By Jack Petrilli

DISCLAIMERS and AUTHOR'S NOTES

This is a work of fiction. Some of the characters are historical, but most of the main ones are fictional. Many of the main events are historical, such as the death of Tiberius. The events dealing with Sylvia and Marcellus are fictional. The names of towns, cities, and roads portrayed are historically accurate.

In many cases, I used the Roman names for common items, such as gladius instead of sword, pugio instead of dagger, and coupana instead of inn or tavern. Any confusion about certain terms can be solved with a simple Internet search.

The somewhat unusual theory that the invention of unbreakable glass might have been seen as a threat by Tiberius to the stability of the Roman currency, was put forth by some historians, and not my original idea.

Finally, to any of you who have made the journey from 31 CE to our present time, I apologize for any inaccuracies portrayed. I did my best to be historically accurate.

Chapter 1

Rome 31 CE

Atticus Ramius Tanaquil was excited and apprehensive at the same time. He had been summoned for an audience with the Emperor Tiberius himself. He could hardly believe it. The glassmaker suspected it had something to do with his invention of flexible, unbreakable glass. Despite his status as a lowly plebeian, he had been treated with all the respect and honor of an important patrician.

He had been picked up at his workshop by a troop of five legionnaires who, perceiving his wariness, had assured him he was not in any trouble. He had been transported by carriage to Sorrento and then put on a sailing ship for the three-mile journey to the island of Capri, which had become the Emperor's permanent residence since 26 CE. Tiberius had never really wanted to be Emperor so his retreating to the Isle of Capri was not all that surprising. He basically allowed Sejanus, the prefect of the Praetorian Guard, to be the de facto ruler in his place.

Physically, there was nothing extraordinary about Atticus. He stood about five feet five which was pretty average for a man of his era. He had dark brown hair and had started to develop a pot belly, again, not so unusual for a man in his late 30s.

Despite the legionnaires' assurances, Atticus was wary, because a trip to Capri was often a death sentence. Tiberius Julius Caesar was a dangerous Emperor, known for his propensity to execute people for the slightest of imagined infractions. The future Emperor Caligula was convinced he was going to be executed when he was summoned to Capri in 31 CE. Tiberius was about five foot eleven with short cropped blondish hair and the classical Roman nose. He had a surly disposition and was not well-liked by the Roman public. A failed assassination attempt had resulted in his permanent move to the island of Capri in 26 CE.

Despite his expectations, Atticus was not brought to any throne room. Instead, he was led to a small but well-furnished room, somewhere in the top floor of Tiberius's palace.

"The Emperor shall see you within the hour. It is expected that you have brought an example of your invention as instructed," said an impressive looking tribune with the faintest hint of distaste.

The tribune's scarcely concealed attitude did not help matters. Atticus fought back the fear that was rising inside of him. "I will be ready," he quavered.

The next hour or so was not very pleasant for Atticus. *I should've tried to run away. Yet, there were five of them. How far could I have gotten?* He became more and more convinced he would never leave this palace alive.

Finally, the same haughty tribune appeared at his door. "If you would follow me," he commanded. Atticus was led through the palace. He marveled at the luxury and opulence evident. All the floors were marble. Colorful statues of gods, goddesses, and heroes were plentiful. His amazement temporarily replaced his terror. Finally, he was led to a very ornate balustrade where sat the man himself, Tiberius. The view from here was spectacular. He was mesmerized at the site of the deep blue Tyrrhenian Sea, to the point where Tiberius had to clear his throat to get Atticus's attention.

Atticus sank to his knees. "Caesar," he shakily voiced.

"Now, now. No need for such formality, Attius," the Emperor remonstrated.

"A-Atticus," the trembling man corrected.

Tiberius frowned and just stared at Atticus.

Atticus gulped. *Maybe I shouldn't have corrected the Emperor. What was I thinking!*

Tiberius quickly resumed his paternal expression. "Atticus, such a beautiful day. I so enjoy being outside on a day like this."

Somewhat surprised at this non sequitur, Atticus managed, "Yes, Caesar. It is indeed a beautiful day."

"Now, my dear fellow, I have heard whispers that you have developed a new process of glassmaking. Is this correct?"

"Yes, Caesar," Atticus answered, unsuccessfully hiding a little of the pride he felt at having done so.

"I have also heard the glass produced is most unusual, that it is unbreakable. Is this true?"

"Yes, Caesar."

"Have you brought me an example of this?"

"Yes, Caesar, I have." Atticus fumbled at a small sack he had carried with him. He finally extracted a medium-sized glass goblet.

"May I see it, Atticus?" Tiberius asked, suspiciously over-polite.

Atticus handed it over. The Emperor turned it over, this way and that. Finally, he flicked it with this fingernail. "As far as I can see, this is just ordinary glass."

"May I have it back, Caesar?" Atticus said, almost afraid to ask.

Tiberius handed the glass back. Atticus raised the glass high and flung it to the marble floor. To everyone's amazement, the glass did not break. It showed the slightest of dents which, even more amazingly, slowly began to disappear as the goblet regained its former shape.

"Why, that is astounding!" exclaimed the Emperor, clearly impressed. "How is this even possible?"

Atticus began to launch into a detailed explanation of the process involved.

"Atticus. Stop," the Emperor commanded. "It was a rhetorical question. I am not interested in the process of glassmaking. It is enough to know this invention exists." He paused, and then continued, "Does anyone else know of this process? I mean to say, have you shared the intricacies of this process with anyone else?"

"No, Caesar. Was I wrong not to do so? I was anticipating financial benefits coming from the sharing of this process." He gulped, "I hope I did not offend in thinking this way."

"No, not at all. Indeed, you were very wise to keep this process a secret." He looked kindly at the glassmaker. "You are dismissed for the time being. We shall talk further on this matter a little later on."

Atticus departed quickly, visibly relieved that nothing untoward had happened to him. Once he was gone, Tiberius turned to the tribune. "Summon Sejanus. I need to talk to him."

Sejanus was Tiberius's second-in-command and actual ruler of Rome at this point. He was also the Emperor's main hitman, being responsible for the many executions that had lately befallen Rome. It took an entire day for Sejanus to arrive from Rome.

What can be so important that the old bastard has to call me away from Rome? This is very inconvenient and only adds to my belief that something has to be done about him. And sooner rather than later. Sejanus fumed upon docking at the Isle of Capri.

He was led to the main throne room where Tiberius always received Sejanus, hoping to quash any seditious ideas. The majesty and opulence of this room was intended to cower any supplicants. Tiberius was cognizant of the dangers involved, allowing someone else to rule in his place. Such was his hatred of being Emperor. He much preferred the days when he was a general of the Army, subduing the tribes of Germania. Indeed, he was a much better general than Emperor.

"You summoned me, Caesar?" Sejanus was careful to appear respectful. He had Tiberius's favor which meant he was currently the de facto Emperor, or at least, co-emperor and he didn't want to do anything to spoil this. It required a delicate juggling act, something Sejanus was eminently capable of doing.

"I seek your advice on an interesting development, Sejanus." The Emperor proceeded to brief Sejanus on Atticus and his invention. When he was finished, Sejanus grew thoughtful. "It is a marvelous invention, Caesar, but I fear it has the potential to destabilize our financial markets. It could lead to the devaluation of gold and silver and as you well know, the royal treasury is mostly made up of gold and silver. There is a possibility this glass would become a second, unofficial currency. Not likely, but possible.”

“Your thoughts mirror mine exactly, Sejanus.”

“Has the glassmaker shared his invention with anyone else, Caesar?”

“Fortunately, he has not.”

“Then the solution is simple.” Sejanus gave the Emperor a significant look.

“My thoughts exactly. See that it is done.”

It had been over a day since Atticus had been summoned to see the Emperor. Finally, four legionnaires appeared at his door. Without saying a single word, two of them grabbed his arms while another slipped a noose around his neck, and strangled him to death. His last thought was, I knew it! *I was right to fear being called to see the Emperor. I should’ve run when I had the chance.*

Chapter 2

Virginia 2021

The trip up Tegar's long driveway often evoked memories in Chuck. How different his life had become since the first time he traveled up it. He chuckled, thinking how he had considered Tegar crazy when he first heard about time travel. He had made some lame excuse to try and leave, but fortunately, Tegar had convinced him to hear him out. He never would have met Anna. He never would have met Abby. He often wondered how it was possible to love two women at the same time. Though she had passed on, his feelings for Anna never did. Tegar had been wise to ban him from the laboratory in the two years before he had met Abby. There was no doubt in his mind whatsoever, he would have tried to return to Anna in 1940s Poland, probably killing himself in the process. He simply did not have the requisite knowledge to activate the time warp safely. Like one of those geek technicians had joked, he probably would've ended up in outer space without a space suit.

And then he had met Abby, or Abigail Trenholm as she had first announced herself. She was now his wife. Sometimes he felt guilty about that, but Anna had lived a full life and died a billionaire at the age of 93, two years before he had even met Abby. The vagaries of time travel. He had only known Anna when she was 20 back in World War II Poland. In a way it was a godsend that she had passed away before Chuck had met Abby. Such was the depths of their feelings for each other, that he was quite sure it would have hurt Anna to learn of his marriage to Abby, despite her advanced age. What could have been, but never was. Anna had sacrificed her chance to be with Chuck in order to save his life. If they had had five more seconds, their lives together would have happened. Men plan and God laughs. Chuck just sighed. Abby was very different than Anna, yet his love for her was as deep and profound as that for Anna.

Chuck proceeded through Tegar's mansion and down the stairs to his laboratory where he found Sylvia and Tegar discussing some item or other. Sylvia noticed his arrival. "Hi Chuck," she beamed.

"And how is my favorite harlot," Chuck replied.

Sylvia just sighed and ignored the friendly jibe as usual. *Is he ever going to get over this and stop teasing me about it?* "How are you and that wonderful wife of yours?" she asked.

Chuck just smiled. "We're doing really well. Abby is adjusting amazingly well to our time and culture. She no longer refuses to go to the beach. And she no longer sneers at women in shorts."

Sylvia just laughed. Chuck was half joking of course and making reference to the time when Abby first met her. She had called Sylvia a harlot, based on the modern 21st-century way Sylvia was dressed. Abby had not yet seen any other 21st-century woman and thus was not aware that Sylvia's dress was normal.

"Oh, and she sends you her regards too. She asked me when you plan on coming over again. She enjoyed our dinner together last week immensely."

"As did I," Sylvia enthused.

It's funny how we almost simultaneously hated each other when we first met. Now she's one of our best friends, thought Chuck, musing about Sylvia. *And probably my best student.*

Sylvia was a tall and lithe red head, lean but shapely, though not quite voluptuous. It wasn't obvious, but she was pretty athletic also, regularly beating Chuck at Squash. Striking blue eyes completed her appearance.

Chuck's duties at Tegar Industries were now exclusively focused on training. Chuck suspected that Tegar had decided not to send him on any more dangerous missions. He would've been correct in that assumption as Tegar secretly considered him the son he had never had.

"So, Sylvia, tomorrow's the big day. I bet you can hardly wait," Chuck said.

She laughed. "You got that right! Six months of studying Latin almost killed me. Did you know there was a difference between church Latin and the Latin spoken during the time of the Romans? As an example, there is no soft 'c' or 'j' in ancient Latin. Julius Caesar would've been pronounced 'Ee-oo-lee-us Kay-zar,' which was where we get the modern words Kaiser and Tsar. They both claimed to come from the Roman empire. All that work, but it was worth it!" She now spoke Latin fluently.

Tegar began, "I got the three of us together as part of a final briefing for tomorrow's mission. Allow me to recapitulate what we already know. Sylvia will be traveling back to 31 CE, our most ambitious project given the amount of time travelled. She is to attempt to find a specimen of the so-called unbreakable glass. Her first objective will be to see if this glassmaking invention actually ever existed. It is quite possible that this unbreakable glass was just a myth. If it does exist, the process has never been replicated. Oh, I know we have fiberglass, etc. but this so-called invention was supposed to be different in some significant ways which we will explore if we ever acquire a specimen. More specifically, if damaged, this glass was supposed to be able to resume its original shape. I don't think I have to tell you that if it does indeed exist, and is significantly different from fiberglass, there is enormous financial potential with it."

He paused and looked at Sylvia. "If it is not a myth, you need to track down where it came from. I don't expect the glassmaker will share his process with you. So, you merely have to obtain a specimen. If it looks like plastic, don't bother bringing it back. Even a new process for developing plastic would have little value."

Tegar turned to Chuck. "Here's the part that's going to surprise you, Chuck, but which Sylvia already knows. She is not going to hide her appearance. We are going to try to make her arrival in front of a local shopkeeper look like the appearance of a goddess."

"Fuck, Tegar! Isn't that a little bit dangerous?" Chuck exclaimed.

Tegar chuckled. "I thought you'd say that, so I saved myself weeks of argument by not telling you about this until the last minute."

"Wouldn't it be better to appear undetected?" Tegar remained silent. Chuck turned to Sylvia. "And you're okay with this?"

"Perfectly. It's not like the Middle Ages. I won't be burned at the stake as a witch. And even if this were a possibility, I would just activate my return to our time. And also, Chuck, Tegar has provided me with a number of safeguards. All Roman women wore an ankle length tunic. The wealthier ones wore a stola over the tunic. I will be dressed that way seeing as I'm supposed to be a goddess. However, my stola and tunic are special. The inside part of the tunic that touches my skin is insulated. The outside part contains a cleverly disguised electrical circuit. I merely have to say, "Computer, activate defense," in English of course, and the circuit becomes live. Anyone touching me at this point would receive a nasty, but nonfatal charge if I release him soon enough. This is for purposes of self-defense and to reinforce the idea that I am a goddess, the goddess Antevorte to be exact. She is a minor goddess, the goddess of the future." She smiled. "Appropriate, don't you think?"

"But- "Chuck started to say.

"That's not all, Chuck. I will have a mirror that corresponds to the watch you had on Anna's mission. Just like yours, it will contain a computer and the means to get back home. It will also have that long-lasting battery, over 50 years of life I believe, that Tegar industries invented but haven't released. Unlike yours, it will respond to two different commands. One will be just like yours, 'computer.' It will only answer to this command in English which should impress the locals as a language of the gods. The other command will be, 'Jupiter.' It will answer this command in Latin. Facial and voice recognition has also been incorporated but this time, the process is instantaneous, not with any delay like yours was. If anyone else besides me tries to use any of these two command words, it will admonish them in Latin not to attempt to communicate with the gods. As you can see, just like yours, the device will not acknowledge anyone else but me."

Tegar added, "Sylvia will also be provided with a special gun that will only fire if it recognizes her thumbprint on the handle. We are hoping she will never have to use this or if she does, just to impress the natives by destroying a jar or something. Just like with you, we don't want her killing anyone as the consequences to the timeline would be enormous. And there's one final thing, Chuck. The special mirror will also be able to display video from our time. Once again, Sylvia might need this to establish her credentials as a goddess. She will maintain this is a view from the land of the gods."

Tegar looked pretty smug at all the precautions. "Finally, she will have a pouch hidden in her tunic, containing medical supplies such as antibiotics, bandages, etc. We are hoping she never has to use this. And, of course, she has had all the necessary vaccinations like you did before you traveled."

Tegar looked at Chuck again. "Do you have anything to add?"

Chuck sighed. "I still think it's pretty dangerous. However, we all signed up for this. We knew the danger, so really there's not much more I can say."

He turned to Sylvia. "There are a few things I can tell you because I'm the only one who's experienced it. Your transformation will be instantaneous. One second, you're here, and the next second you're at your destination. If you appear right in front of this shopkeeper, step back at first. There is no telling what his first surprised reaction will be. He may try to attack you."

Sylvia smiled at him. She knew his concern for her was genuine. Chuck continued. "Sylvia, everything will appear different to you. The air will smell differently. The lighting will be different. I found this very jarring. It will seem incredibly quiet. We are so accustomed to background noise in our modern lives. These may seem like little differences when explained, but they're not when experienced. What I found most surprising were the people. You will find they are mostly like us, but also different in ways you will find disconcerting. I tell you this so you won't show any kind of surprise when you arrive, seeing as you're gonna be standing right in front of a local. If you are to be a goddess, you should not be non-plussed at appearing in front of this man. I suspect you should act a bit haughty."

They both grinned at this, remembering their first encounter, when Sylvia had been quite haughty. *I wonder if he realizes how many times he has warned me about these things,* she mused.

Tegar finally added, "I don't think I need to remind you that you will reappear in our time five minutes after you left, no matter how long you spend in the past." He smiled. "So, don't be surprised if we act a little shocked at your reappearance, especially if you've spent a long time in the past. You probably will look quite different to us than five minutes ago."

Sylvia just smiled ruefully. It's not like she hadn't heard most of this millions of times in the last several weeks. She entered the time machine. There was a slight hum and she was gone.

"One thing I've often wondered about, Malcolm. Why do you have us return five minutes after we leave?" Chuck asked.

"Simple. If the time traveler doesn't return after five minutes, I know something bad happened and we have to send someone else in to find out if our first traveler is alive or in trouble. In this particular case, Chuck, that would be you," Tegar answered.

Chuck smiled ruefully. "Yeah, I figured that. Let's hope this won't be necessary."

Chapter 3

Rome 31 CE

Marcellus Pontius Silanus was not having a good day. Sales at his wine shop had been abysmal. Not even the cheap Lora or Posca had sold well. He looked out at the pouring rain that had been going on all day and sighed. *I suppose I shouldn't be surprised. Who wants to be out on a day like this? Still, I shouldn't complain. Up until today, business has been really good,* he thought, looking around his shop at the collection of dolia, amphora, and glass bottles around him.

He decided to close up early. *No sense trying to kick a dead horse.* He summoned his slave, Marcipor, to help him. He cleared off the counter used for serving customers who only wanted a single glass. He then stoppered his open bottles of Lora, Posca, and Mulsum. He only sold the more expensive Falernian by bottle or amphora. He was one of the few merchants who were wealthy enough to keep the much larger dolia in his shop, the only disadvantage being needing help from Marcipor to pour from the dolia to the smaller amphoras. This saved him from having to access his suppliers as often as some of his competitors. It also gave him the flexibility to order when the price was most advantageous. He closed and locked the shutters to his shop, but couldn't help looking around in satisfaction one more time before retiring to his living space in the back. *Not bad for this old soldier,* he thought. Marcellus was actually only 37 years old.

Even though he had no family, Marcellus' living quarters were quite spacious. He had lost his wife and his child to the plague three years ago. His Pater Familias had granted him his freedom, as was customary, just before he entered the Army. So all his possessions were indeed his. He even had a small courtyard and a personal latrine which emptied out to a stream flowing below. This was quite rare for a shopkeeper, but Marcellus had been doing very well since his stint as a soldier. He was no patrician, but he lived as some of the less wealthy ones did.

The rain stopped an hour later and the late afternoon sun came out. *Maybe I closed up too early,* he ruefully thought. *Ah well, I can use a little time off now and then.* Marcipor was in the kitchen, getting their meal ready.

Marcellus decided to sit out in his little courtyard and enjoy what little daylight was left. And that is the precise moment when his world went to hell.

Suddenly, a tall, red haired beauty appeared in front of him, seemingly out of thin air. She was wearing a white tunic with the aristocratic stola over it. Marcellus was stunned and almost fell out of his chair. "Marcipor, come hither," he quavered loudly.

Marcipor did not miss the note of urgency in his master's voice. He hurried in and stopped abruptly, stunned by the appearance of Sylvia. "B-but, how? The shutters were closed and locked. How did you get in?"

She looked down at the two of them haughtily. "I am the goddess Antevorte and I require your service." This in a high, contralto voice.

Marcellus slowly got over his shock and began to inspect her. He had rarely seen a woman taller than his five foot eight but she was clearly taller, though not by much. She had flaming red hair and he hadn't seen skin so fair since fighting the German tribes up north. Her eyes were an incredible shade of blue. She was lean but sexy as all hell as far as he was concerned. What amazed him most was her level of cleanliness. No dust or splotches of dirt anywhere. *Is she indeed a goddess? I never really believed in the gods.* Then, *the home of the gods must be very clean*, he thought incongruously.

He finally began to consider what she had said. *I have a business to run. I don't have time to help her, goddess or no goddess.* His business was always of paramount importance to him.

There was no doubt that he was afraid. But he had been a soldier. He had faced death many times. He refused to be cowed now. "If you are a goddess, why do you need the help of a lowly man like me?"

This was completely surprising to Sylvia who had expected a groveling, terrified man. She shouldn't have been, had she known the kind of man Marcellus was. He had fought bravely against the Germanic tribes. He had seen, more than any man should, the horrors of war. He was not easily frightened and tended to be calm, cool, and collected when faced with any threat.

"That is not your concern, human. Your concern is to obey," she said in as haughty a voice as she could manage.

"And if I don't," he challenged.

Sylvia sighed. *I've only been here a minute and a show of force is already required.* She retrieved the gun from her stola. She pointed it at a small statue which she assumed must represent one of his household gods. She fired. Marcellus jumped at the loud bang as the statute exploded into large fragments.

He looked up at her in shock and dismay. *She really is a goddess and I'm going to have to obey, dammit.*

Just then, Marcipor fell to his knees. He needed no further proof of her divinity. "Marcellus, I heard thunder and then the statue shattered." He stopped, not even daring to look at Sylvia. "Marcellus, by all the gods, you must obey."

Sylvia ignored Marcipor for the time being, realizing by his dress that he must be a slave. She continued to gaze at Marcellus. "What is your name, human?"

"You are a goddess. Don't you already know my name?" he sneered. Marcellus simply refused to be cowed, even though, if truth be told, he was terrified.

"Impertinence," she calmly replied and started to aim the gun at another statue.

"NO! NO! DON'T," he shouted in panic. "Marcellus Pontius Silanus is my name, and this is my slave, Marcipor. I am at your service." Marcellus wondered why the household god whose statue she had destroyed, had not reacted. *I never really believed in the gods but perhaps some do exist,* he mused, looking at her with newfound respect.

She smiled in victory at him and he grimaced, not caring at all that her smile was perfect with her dazzlingly white teeth. *Sure, she's beautiful, but this is going to be a pain in the ass.*

Marcipor had heard his master say 'Goddess'." He remained on his knees and whimpered, "As am I."

"Are you a glassblower, Marcellus?"

"No, I own a wine shop," he said, hoping this would disqualify him from her service if it was a glassblower she needed.

She frowned. *Well, the odds were pretty low that I'd be that lucky. I guess I should consider myself fortunate they were able to place me inside any shop at all. Sometimes it boggles my mind how good Tegar's technicians are.*

Unknown to Sylvia, the technicians had spent days mulling over old surviving maps of ancient Rome, finally choosing a rather large shop that had its own courtyard. Least chance of a disastrous mistake this way, though they hoped beyond hope she would successfully reappear five minutes later. So many things could go wrong with a journey this far back into the past. Sylvia had been warned this trip was not nearly as safe as the previous two involving Chuck had been. She did not realize how grateful she should've been, not appearing inside a wall or in outer space.

Sylvia studied the two men. *Hmmm, Marcellus is slightly taller than what I've been led to believe was common for this era. Pretty well-built, too. Olive complexioned skin. Rugged features and a slight scar on his chin. Maybe a former soldier. Cleaner than I would've imagined. Even his teeth seem to be in good shape, probably due to his sugarless Mediterranean diet, and I did read most Romans brushed their teeth with some kind of stick or branch, I think.*

Marcipor is smaller and fairer. He could be Gaelic or Celtic. Relations between master and slave seem to be good. He called Marcellus by his name and not 'master.'

"Show me your abode," she commanded.

"Don't the gods see from on high?" He sneered again.

She started to reach for her gun. "No need! I'll do as you say!" He
exclaimed in a panic and then sighed in defeat.

She regarded him coldly. *Damn, just my luck, I had to get a brave Roman.
I would've preferred snivelling terror.*

He took her on a tour of his house. She was surprised at how colorful
everything was. The many murals and statues were not the plain white of
the ruins that existed in her day. They were all colorfully painted.

All of the rooms opened either to the interior or to the courtyard. None of
them opened to the outside. The shuttered atrium, which was the first part
of the house, was connected to his shop by a small, narrow passageway,
only about 12 feet in length.

She was shocked and dismayed at the latrine. It was not in a separate
room. It was open to the whole house. There was also a large sponge at
the end of the stick, presently immersed in a jar of vinegar. It was pretty
obvious what this was for seeing as they had no toilet paper which to her,
was thoroughly disgusting and not very hygienic.

"Your latrine," she began, pausing to think of a polite way to say this.

Marcellus jumped in. "Yes, we have our own. No need to use the public
ones," he beamed proudly.

"Ummm, what I mean to say is that you have to place a curtain in front of it.
I do not wish anybody to be able to see-"

"The gods have need of a latrine?!" He was genuinely shocked, and a
glimmering of suspicion started to creep in.

"Yes, we do," she nonchalantly answered. "In many ways, the gods are
just like humans. We also sleep. I shall have need of your sleeping
quarters while here. You will move to Marcipor's quarters. Also, your room
has no door. A curtain shall be placed at the entrance there."

*No doubt she needs a curtain to hide the fact that she turns into a demon
when unobserved,* he exasperatedly thought.

"Finally, I need to bathe every second day. You or your slave need to fill the tub with warm water for this."

"I only bathe at home once a week," he grumbled.

She sniffed. "Yes, I can tell."

He ignored the insult. "Can you not use the public baths? It requires a fair amount of work to fill the tub with warm water."

"I am aware, Marcellus. I cannot use the public baths. It would become obvious that I am not human, and I wish to remain anonymous."

Marcellus frowned deeply. *Maybe she really does turn into a demon. Bossy bitch, and her Latin is atrocious. Do the gods not have proper instructors?* He considered some more. *What would become obvious anyway? She may be a goddess, but she looks like a human in every respect. She needs to use the toilet. She needs to sleep. Something is off here, even if she did appear out of thin air. I'm not willing to give up my disbelief of the gods quite yet.*

Sylvia felt a bit of sympathy for him. She was upending his life after all. "Marcellus, do not be so vexed. With a little luck, I shall not be here long."

That is indeed a blessing, he ruefully thought, once again oblivious to her beauty.

Chapter 4

Rome 31 CE The next day

The early morning sun shone brightly. *No rain today,* thought Marcellus with some relief. *Now the question is, will she allow me to go about my business?* He looked over at Sylvia. She was standing in the middle of the courtyard seemingly lost in contemplation. *I need to get a better feel for this place before I start my search.*

Some things just don't make sense, he mused. *Sure, she's some kind of supernatural being. No doubt about that. I should add, a really beautiful supernatural being. But how can she be a Roman goddess? She doesn't look Roman at all. She is fair skinned and very tall. Truth be told, she looks like a German or a Gaul. And she speaks Latin like a foreigner. Is it possible that she's some kind of German goddess, pretending to be Roman? And if this is so, could her mission be something nefarious to Rome? Does helping her make me a traitor? And am I starting to believe in the gods?*

Sylvia startled him out of his reverie. "Marcellus, I would like you to show me more of Rome before we proceed on our search for this glassblower."

"A tour of Rome? Goddess, ummm Antevorte, I need to run my business. Surely you can see that?" He implored. *Shouldn't she already know what Rome looks like? This is getting more and more suspicious.*

"Marcipor will be running things today," she haughtily answered.

Marcellus persisted. "Could not Marcipor show you our city?"

"Yes, I suppose he could. But it shall be you who will perform this task." Seeing his chagrin, she continued, "I foresee fewer problems if I am accompanied by a wealthy citizen, rather than by a slave."

"Alright, your highness," he sneered angrily.

She smiled at him which only increased his fury. "No need to get prickly," she admonished.

If she's a Roman goddess, shouldn't she know all about Rome? He worried again. Things were getting murkier and murkier as far as Marcellus was concerned.

"Oh, and before I forget, how often do you change the bucket of vinegar in the latrine?" she innocently asked.

He looked at her strangely, finding her question somewhat weird. She was looking at him expectantly. "Once a week, like everyone else," he muttered.

Christ, once a week! she ruefully thought. "Marcellus, from now on, you will change the vinegar in that bucket every single day."

"You must think money grows on trees," he angrily retorted. "First, I'm not allowed to run my business, and now this!"

She smiled at him again and then reached into her stola and produced a gold Aureus. "I believe this is worth about a month's wages for the common citizen, probably a little less for you." She handed him the coin. He studied it distrustfully, turning it over and over. It had the picture of Augustus on one side, and the picture of a bull on the other. *This seems genuine, but why does it look so old? And why not a coin of Tiberius? They are so much more common nowadays.*

"Can we proceed now?" She asked smugly.

He grunted his assent. *She really is a bossy bitch! Typical of my luck that she picked me,* he ruefully thought.

Reading about Roman life, and seeing it firsthand, are two very different things, she discovered. The physical street itself was somewhat monotonous. All the stucco shops appeared the same when shuttered. The biggest difference was that there were no windows facing outward like on a modern street. The street itself was paved with what seemed to her to be flat stones sealed in concrete.

She looked about her. The street was starting to fill with shoppers, merchants, and soldiers. Surprisingly to her, there were lots of women about, some without any male companionship. From her studying, she knew this would have been impossible in ancient Greece. Some of the Roman women wore stolas, which indicated they were either married or wealthy or both. Others only had their tunics which indicated a lower status in life. Not all the men wore togas. It appeared that laboring men did not wear them at all. Instead, they wore knee length tunics with cloaks over their shoulders.

The smell was something else. She had learned that the Romans were relatively clean and their streets weren't as bad as later medieval times. This might have been true, but the streets still smelled. Despite the existence of public latrines and the Roman practice of usually emptying their chamber pots into these latrines, some still just threw their waste into the street. Combine this with the smell of horses and the numerous dogs running about and you got a pretty unpleasant aroma which the natives didn't even seem to notice. Being a product of the 21st century, Sylvia noticed.

Marcellus noted her distaste. "What seems to be the problem, your highness?"

She became annoyed and spoke quietly to her reluctant companion. "Marcellus, I do not wish anyone to know who I really am. Do not address me that way again, even in jest, or there will be consequences. Perhaps you should treat me as your wife."

Thank the heavens that isn't the real case, although there would be certain aspects of that I wouldn't mind, he thought ruefully.

Despite her wish to remain inconspicuous, Sylvia was noticed by many, especially by the males. Her height, fair skin, and hair color made this inevitable. Most probably assumed she was German or Gaelic. Roman wives were treated with great respect by the Romans, so no one made forward or lewd remarks to her, but a couple did wink at Marcellus, displaying their envy. The ones who actually knew Marcellus were mystified. They knew he wasn't married, so where did this woman come from? Some tried to stop him and engage in conversation but she subtly pulled him along, indicating he should ignore these requests.

"They will think I am rude," he complained.

"So how would you explain my presence?" She remonstrated. "I don't look like you, so they would know I couldn't be a relative. They probably know you're not married. If you have a girlfriend, I am obviously not her. So, what would you say, Marcellus?"

He sighed. "I guess you've made your point." Still angry at being corrected by her impeccable logic, he added, "Perhaps I could say you are a German slave I captured years ago and have been hiding away all these years for sexual purposes."

This only annoyed her more. Sylvia worked at composing herself. She knew the Romans were very liberal when it came to sexual matters, but she also knew this was an intended jibe. "Careful, Marcellus. I may find it necessary to discipline you, and if I do, you won't like it," she warned.

He looked intensely at her, completely unafraid. She couldn't help but admire his pluck. *This guy should be terrified of me. Yet he's not. You have to give him credit. I just hope this doesn't cause problems down the line.*

They proceeded down the Via Apia until they arrived at a large rectangular building. "That's the Circus Maximus, isn't it, Marcellus?"

"Yes, it is. Do you like chariot racing?"

"Not really. But I am curious. Maybe someday," she responded. "I would like to see the Roman Forum. I believe it's on the Via Sacra, isn't it?"

"Right again, Antevorte. Not that far away neither." *So, she knows of the existence of the Forum and Circus Maximus, but she obviously had never seen them before. She is no Roman goddess, that is for sure. But then, what is she? A foreign goddess? A threat to Rome? Yet what kind of threat would be looking for a glassblower?*

The Via Sacra was the main street of ancient Rome. The road was part of the traditional route of the Roman Triumph. The road was also used for the funeral processions of the emperors.

She couldn't help but be impressed upon arrival at the Forum. These were not the ruins she had once visited. These were beautiful, large official buildings, like the Curia Julia, built by Julius Caesar, where the Senate now met. There were also many temples, arches, and basilicas there. She knew better than to ask about the Roman Coliseum. It wouldn't be built for another 50 years.

After spending a couple of hours there, getting a feel for the vibrant Roman Forum, she asked to see a poor neighborhood.

"Whatever for?" Marcellus asked, genuinely perplexed and a little surprised.

"I need to get a feel for all of Rome, not just the grand parts." In truth, she was just being a tourist, but she couldn't see any harm in it, and this was an opportunity not to be wasted.

He sighed, "Well then, I'll take you to Surbia. But I must caution you. It might be a little dangerous."

She looked at him with a blank expression. "You forget who I am. I am in no danger from anything your world can produce." Sylvia knew that ancient Rome in this period did not have any active police force. These neighborhoods were largely controlled by criminal gangs, but she was confident in the defense items Tegar had provided for her.

Surbia was close to the center of the city. People lived in poorly structured three-story wooden apartments. Poverty and crime were rampant. The odor here was much worse than in the more prosperous areas as people were more apt to empty their chamber pots on the street. Somewhat surprisingly, there did exist local bars where men could go to drink and gamble. And these usually stayed open at night, unlike the shops in the more affluent regions.

It was dusk and the sun was starting to go down. Marcellus looked around warily. "If I had known you wanted to come to a place like this, I would've brought my sword," he grumbled.

"Are you afraid, Marcellus?" she taunted.

He gave her a prison stare look. "Not afraid, but wary. Only a fool wouldn't be."

Marcellus' warning proved to have some merit as they were approached by two thugs who had noticed their well-to-do dress. "Things will go easier for you if you just hand over your valuables," one of them threatened.

"Hold on there, Claudius," he said, looking over Sylvia with narrowed eyes. "This one holds more promise than just valuables."

Sylvia was surprised to see Marcellus move in front of her and take up a belligerent stance. "It's best if you two thugs just move on," he threatened.

He was met with laughter. "And just what do you think you can do, grandpa."

Marcellus started to move forward. Claudius pulled a large knife and advanced on Marcellus.

"Marcellus, stay back. I can handle this," she whispered urgently. "Make sure you don't touch me for the next few minutes." He looked at her in dismay, completely confused.

"But these men are dangerous," he hissed.

"Stay back, I say. That is a command. I said I can handle this."

She then commanded in English, "Computer, activate defense." Her specially designed electrical shield turned on. Both men looked at her strangely, wondering what language this was. She turned to Claudius's companion. "What is your name, miscreant? I need to know your name before I punish you."

Once again, this elicited laughter. "My name is Marius, lady, and I don't think I'm the one who's going to be punished," he scoffed. He advanced on her. With a lascivious smile, he reached out and put his hand on her. There was a snap and a crackle as 200 volts surged through his body. She did not wish to kill him, very aware of the mandate not to change the timeline. So she flung him to the ground, breaking the circuit. He might not have been dead but he looked that way as he lay unconscious on the ground.

I need to play this right, she mused. "Jupiter, I am grateful for the power thou hast endowed in me," she intoned in an older form of Latin, thinking in some amusement, *Tegar would probably be very pleased to be called 'Jupiter.'* The remaining man, eyes widened, was staring at her in amazement. She turned to Claudius. "Begone!" She commanded. He needed no further prompting as he took off running.

Marcellus started to reach for her. "STOP!" She commanded urgently. "I told you not to touch me right now. Did you not see what just happened?" she remonstrated ruefully. "Computer, deactivate defense," she hastily added.

"I had my doubts, Antevorte, but now I can see you are indeed a goddess. Was that the language of the gods I just heard?"

"Yes," she answered simply, wondering at the slight unease she felt at his newfound conviction.

"Is this what will happen to me if I touch you?"

"No. Only if I call on my powers. I will warn you beforehand if I should do so. It is safe now."

He put his hand on her shoulder. "I am glad you are safe." And he really was, which was somewhat surprising to both of them.

She just looked at him and wondered.

Chapter 5

Rome 31 CE The next day

Marcellus was very chagrined. "You do realize there could be as many as 50 different glassblowers in Rome, don't you? And you don't even know the name of the one you seek."

"Yet, but how many of them can claim to have invented unbreakable glass?" She replied icily. *Is this guy going to be difficult about everything? She wondered. Couldn't they have sent me to someone a little bit more amenable? His good looks just don't compensate for this bullshit!*

He sighed, "Admittedly, I have never heard of this. Are you certain this invention exists?" *The gods are playing with me. Send me someone beautiful who is driving me crazy.*

"No," she replied simply.

He gaped at her. "Then why are we going to be searching for something that might not even exist?"

"That is part of my mission, Marcellus, first to ascertain if this even exists. And if it does, to acquire the formula in building it."

"Hah! Are you telling me the gods do not have this capability? Or can they not even tell from high up whether this exists or not?"

Not having an easy answer, she ignored the second question. "We do not have the capability. We do have something called fiberglass. But this substance can be shattered with enough force. The item we're seeking apparently just bends when struck, and then resumes its former shape. Why would I be here if we already have the type of glass I'm seeking?"

"So the gods are not all-powerful as we have been taught."

"No, I suppose we are not. But we are more powerful than you." She looked at him significantly. "In any event, I am not going to argue this any further. My lot is to command and yours is to obey. I've had enough of this banter. We shall begin our quest."

This certainly did not please Marcellus. It was almost as if his manhood was being called into question. But he had seen what she had done to that thug and decided discretion was better than valor.

He sighed. "Marcipor you are in charge of the shop once again." *It's a damn good thing I have probably the most trustworthy slave in Rome,* he exasperatedly thought.

A few days passed with little result. Marcellus was getting a little frustrated at the time lost for his business. Sylvia was beginning to respect him more and more. For one thing, she didn't notice his smell anymore, even though he only bathed once a week. She knew he wasn't using the public baths because he was with her almost all of the time. He had already demonstrated his bravery. And she couldn't help notice he was friendly and polite with his neighbors. It was pretty obvious they all liked him also.

Despite his frustration, Marcellus was also learning to respect Sylvia more. Though a goddess, she never flaunted her power needlessly. Though she had been a bit bossy at first, she treated him with politeness and respect. It didn't hurt that she was absolutely gorgeous, but unlike many beauties he had known, she was not arrogant about this in the least. He was also impressed with the way she treated Marcipor. She was kind to him and treated him as an equal, something not many slaves experienced.

If truth be told, he was becoming attracted to her. *This is utterly ridiculous. She is a goddess. I am a human. Where can this possibly go? I must be careful to hide this attraction for I'm certain she would be insulted if she knew. I don't want to have to deal with an insulted goddess.* He shuddered, thinking again about what had happened to her assailant a few days ago.

That night, he had a vivid dream about her. She had approached him, complaining about a small rip in her toga.

"Take it off and I'll have Marcipor repair it," he offered.

She did so, now only wearing a tunic. He gasped at the beauty of her shape. Full breasts. Tiny waist. Curvaceous hips. She noticed his staring. "Marcellus, is there something I can do for you?" She mischievously asked.

He was stunned as she began removing her tunic. She got completely naked. She was so beautiful and she was approaching him with this intense wanting look on her face… And then he woke up. He pounded his pillow in frustration and tried to go back to sleep to resume his dream. Of course, that didn't work.

She didn't understand why he was a bit grumpy with her first thing in the morning. She thought they had moved past that stage. *And they say women are moody!*

As luck would have it, they hit paydirt that very same day. A butcher shop owner on the Vius Longus had heard of a glassblower who had claimed the new invention. "This idiot claims his glass doesn't break. Pretty stupid, if you ask me," disparaged the butcher.

Marcellus and Sylvia both grew excited. They started to talk over each other. Sylvia gave Marcellus a look. He quieted.

"Good citizen, would you know where this glassblower is located?" She asked.

"Not precisely. In Viminalis for sure. I think he's probably on the Veus Viminalis. That's just one street over," he said as he pointed east.

They couldn't make their way fast enough in their excitement. They hit paydirt on the third place they made inquiries, a candlemaker's shop.

"Oh sure, that would be Atticus's shop. Atticus Ramius Tanaquil to be exact. Just keep going down this road. His will be on the right-hand side, right next to the fruit seller's. What is your business with him?"

They started to talk over each other again. Sylvia gave Marcellus an exasperated look this time. He looked sheepish.

"We would like to see if he really has this special glass. I would be interested in buying some," she lied.

They found the shop within the next five minutes. But it was shuttered, even though it was the middle of the day. Marcellus banged on the shutters, to no avail. The fruit seller came over to see what the commotion was about.

"The owner hasn't been here the last six days," he explained.

"Do you know where he has gone?" asked Sylvia.

"Not really, but I have my suspicions. Five legionnaires showed up here and picked him up. I have no idea where they were taking him, but it didn't look good to me."

Sylvia sighed. *Just my luck! Tiberius got to him just before me.*

Marcellus started trying to force the lock.

"Hey, what are you doing!" shouted the fruit seller.

"It is important we get inside," Sylvia answered coolly.

"Yeah, so you can steal everything of value." The fruit seller looked thoroughly disgusted.

Sylvia turned to him. "I assure you, sir, that is not our intent. You can come inside with us, if you wish. Has Atticus mentioned a new type of glass he may have invented?"

"Yes, he did," answered the fruit seller, somewhat surprised and mollified by the fact that this beautiful woman knew Atticus's name.

"It is important we secure his invention as Atticus is either in a dungeon or dead." The fruit seller stared at her in dismay. He fervently wished this wasn't the case, but he had already suspected that this was so.

Marcellus looked over at Sylvia. *There's more than meets the eye about this damn glass,* he thought. *First, the gods send someone to retrieve it and then someone else, maybe the Emperor himself, thinks it important enough to make the inventor disappear.*

Marcellus was having no luck with the lock. "Stand aside," Sylvia commanded, pulling out her gun. She fired and the lock shattered. The loud bang caused the fruit seller to startle and attracted some attention all down the street.

He looked at Sylvia. "By Jupiter, who are you?" He quavered in a barely audible voice.

"I am the goddess Antevorte and you shall keep this information secret, my little human," she commanded.

The fruit seller was shaking. Marcellus felt a little sympathy for him, remembering how he felt on his first encounter with her. Somehow, he had become quite comfortable with the goddess at his side.

"Am I understood?" she silkily inquired to the fruit seller.

"Yes, Your Majesty," he barely managed. "There is n-no need for me to go inside with you." Marcellus chuckled at the "Your Majesty" part. He couldn't blame the poor sot though.

They spent hours searching the shop. They found plenty of notes, but not one detailing the whole process. Then they threw every bottle they could find to the floor. Every single one of them shattered.

"So, it's just a rumor then. No such thing has been invented," surmised Marcellus.

"I'd like to think so. But then why would someone feel the need to seize him? On the one hand, it would mean I could go home. But I have been tasked with not leaving one single stone unturned, which means we have to find out what happened to Atticus. I just need to make sure before I leave."

Marcellus had mixed feelings. On the one hand, he could return to his daily routine. On the other hand, Antevorte would be gone and, try as he might to deny this, he knew he would miss her.

Chapter 6

Rome 31 CE

"A message from Sejanus, Caesar." The Tribune bowed respectfully and handed the message to Tiberius. The Emperor sighed. *Why does he bother me with these matters? I left him in charge to rule, not pester me with nonsense.*

He almost decided to ignore the message, thinking Sejanus would get the hint and stop bothering him. Yet his curiosity got the better of him, so he opened the scroll. It read:

Caesar, I decided to completely destroy that glassblower's shop. You remember, the one with the unbreakable glass. Unfortunately, my legionnaires report the shop had already been broken into and completely vandalized. A thorough search did not find any indication of the process involved in making that glass. Whoever broke into the shop might have the formula or a sample of the glass itself. Further inquiries of the glassblower's neighbors revealed a man and a woman were the perpetrators. So far, I have not been able to discover their names, but I am continuing my search.

Tiberius heaved a sigh. He called for a scribe and then began dictating, "Sejanus, why do you continue to bother me with these trivialities? Your course of action should have been obvious without my input. Find these two and kill them, after making sure they do not have the formula or the glass."

Meanwhile, back at Marcellus's shop, he and Sylvia were involved in a testy conversation. It had started with Marcellus trying to act nonchalant when he asked Sylvia, "Do goddesses ever marry humans?"

She looked at him morosely. "Marcellus, do not go there," she implored. She had started to feel some attraction to him also, but she knew this was a complete dead end. She was going back to the 21st century, while he would be remaining here.

"Go where?" He asked innocently.

"You know perfectly well, where," she replied with some chagrin.

"Well, you haven't answered my question."

"It would be impossible," finding a way to avoid a direct answer.

"Would be impossible because no goddess would ever desire such? Or is there a law against it? Or would it be physically impossible?"

In her world, Tegar was the law. "There is a law against it."

"But then, it is physically possible. There is only the law that forbids it." He was cornering her and she knew it. To have a man desire her to whom she was also attracted, and to have to extinguish the possibility, was proving to be very difficult. She never could've imagined this sort of problem would come up. She felt a bit guilty about how she reacted to Chuck falling in love with Anna. She had been very disdainful at that time.

He looked into her eyes and read her indecision. He started to close the distance between the two. She knew she would have to put a stop to this right now, before it was too late. "Yes, it is only a law. But I always, listen to me closely Marcellus, I *always* obey the law. You presume too much, human." It almost killed her to say that last part, but she had to discourage him.

He was hurt and angry at the same time. "I presume nothing, goddess. I was only curious." And with that, he stalked out of the room. She wasn't surprised at how dismayed she felt over his reaction.

She sought to distract herself by talking with Marcipor. "How came you to be a slave, Marcipor?"

"I was captured by Marcellus in a battle. I was then forced to take this slave name, Marcipor. My real name is Hardingjar of the Irminones tribe."

"Why, that is awful!" She exclaimed although she knew this was common practice for the time. In fact, it would take another 1900 years before most of the world abolished slavery.

"You know, at first I thought so. I begged Marcellus to kill me. I had no family to support, so it was nothing to me to die. At first, he kept a close eye on me to make sure I didn't do anything untoward. But as time passed on, I came to realize that Marcellus was a fine man and would not take advantage of his status as my master."

"Yes, I can see that. He treats you more like a partner than a slave."

"Yes he does, Majesty. He even pays me a wage. I shall be able to buy my freedom within the next three years. Once that happens, he has given me the option of returning to my tribe in Germania, or remaining here and becoming his true partner, in law as well as in fact. As I have already mentioned, I have no family in Germania. I believe I shall remain here and work towards gaining Roman citizenship. I have already become a Roman in actuality, if not by law. There are many benefits to becoming a Roman citizen."

This did not surprise Sylvia all that much. Roman citizenship was readily available, even to former slaves, just part of the wisdom that allowed the Roman Empire to exist for so long.

That night, a gust of wind extinguished the fire that burned over a sort of clay bowl favored by the Romans for lighting purposes. Sylvia was annoyed by the frequency of this event. "I don't understand why you don't just top this lamp with glass?"

"With glass?" He asked, bemused at what he thought was her ignorance.

"Yes, glass. It would stop the wind from constantly blowing out the flame."

He chuckled. *Could the gods be so ignorant!* "Surely you must know enclosing the flame with glass would snuff out the fire."

"Not if the top of the glass was open-ended," she smirked. "Your lamps would be protected from the wind and still get enough oxygen to burn."

He frowned and grew thoughtful. "Oxygen?" He asked.

"Yes, oxygen. You know, the stuff that allows combustion."

Now he looked totally confused. Sylvia couldn't help laughing. "Never mind, Marcellus. Trust me in this. Have a glassblower make you a slightly rounded bottle, open at both ends, but with one end able to fit in one of your lamps. The wind will no longer be a concern."

Christ, what am I doing? I may have just created a technological advance that shouldn't happen for centuries, and all because I was annoyed. You need to be more careful, Sylvia dear.

He took on that thoughtful look again. "I do believe that would work," he gushed happily. "Is that how the gods use their lamps?"

"No, Marcellus. We used to, but no longer."

"Then how do you light your rooms at night?"

"We use electricity." Seeing his confusion, she added, "We have found a way to capture lightning in a bottle."

"Now you are jesting," he said in obvious disbelief.

She considered. Wasn't she supposed to fortify the idea she was a goddess? What would be the harm? So she pulled out her computer/mirror. "Marcellus, come here please."

He complied quickly, enjoying her scent immensely. She was also a bit distracted by his closeness. "Computer, show us an image of a room lit by a few lamps," she said in English.

"Look into the mirror, Marcellus. What do you see?"

His eyes widened as he took in what he considered a room of the gods. He could see the lamps she was talking about, but he also could see so much more. The room was cleaner than any he had ever seen. The furniture was exquisite. The walls were made of some shiny, smooth substance, and painted in a light blue color. There was no stucco to be seen anywhere. The floor was made of shiny planks of dark wood and covered with a Persian rug.

"Why, this is incredible, Antevorte! It must be the room of a very powerful god."

"On the contrary, Marcellus. This is an ordinary room in an ordinary house owned by a man of middle means." She immediately realized her mistake. "I mean it is owned by a GOD of middle means."

"You must find our world very drab," he muttered, depressed at the thought she would never accept living in his world. *But she did say "man." Why would a goddess make such a mistake? There is something going on here that I can't see. She's hiding something.*

I just did it again! This may have been a mistake, she mused. *Have I inadvertently advanced technology? I mean, I have no idea when people actually figured this out for themselves, although I'm pretty sure it's far in the future from now. This is the exactly the kind of thing Tegar warned me about. I need to be more careful. Chuck would be disappointed to see how many flubs his star pupil has already made.*

A few hours later found Marcellus cooking cena, the Roman equivalent of supper. Initially, he had been surprised that the gods needed to eat it all. However, not only did Antevorte eat, she ate heartily. *Well, she's a tall woman. I guess she needs to eat a lot. However, there's not an ounce of fat on her. If I didn't know better, I'd say she was a Spartan warrior woman.*

Sylvia had not expected the 'semi-feast' Marcellus prepared most nights. Supper usually involved some kind of meat, usually pork, chicken, or fish. She had yet to see any beef. There was always some frumentatio, which was a kind of unmilled wheat bread. Sometimes sweet buns were offered, other times cheesecakes made with ricotta cheese. There was always an assortment of vegetables which were brimming with flavor, much more so than their modern equivalents. Potatoes and tomatoes never made an appearance, however. Sylvia believed these had not yet been discovered. Dessert usually involved fruit such as apples or pears, or wine cakes made with honey, red wine, and cinnamon. Of course, wine accompanied all meals, but water was always added to the wine, making it less potent than what one would encounter in modern times. People actually looked down on anyone who did not water down their wine as being ill bred.

He must make a good living with the wine shop, she concluded. Marcipor helped with the cooking, but it was obvious Marcellus enjoyed the activity, as he did most of it. And he was a good cook. She had yet to taste a meal that wasn't delicious. *There's something to be said about a man who enjoys cooking,* she involuntarily thought. She grew even more thoughtful. *You know, I should really be thinking about leaving. Is trying to find Atticus just an excuse to remain? He's probably dead. I could easily go back and report that the formula is lost if it even existed. Yet, I don't want to. Not yet. When I figure out why, I'll go back. Only five minutes would've elapsed in Tegar's lab after all, so what would be the harm.*

Chapter 7

Rome 31 CE

Within two days, Sejanus's spies had been able to learn the identities of Marcellus and Sylvia. Much questioning had revealed these two had been making lots of enquiries about Atticus. It was a simple matter of putting together two plus two. Four legionnaires were dispatched to arrest the two with instructions not to kill them. They needed to be interrogated. Fortunately for Marcellus, Sylvia was still with him.

"I don't like this. I don't like this at all," complained Sextus. "Marcellus Silanus was my Decanus (Sergeant) in the German campaign and he was a damn fine one. He took care of his men, never forcing us to take unnecessary risks. And now we're supposed to arrest him? What for? I know for a fact he's a good Roman, very patriotic."

"Oh, stop bitching! We're not killing him. We're only arresting him," answered Rustius.

"Yes, only arresting him," replied Sextus sarcastically. "By order of Sejanus, and you very well know what that means. He'll be lucky if he isn't tortured before he's killed."

"Mind yourself, Sextus, or it might be you we're arresting next."

Sextus grumbled but remained silent, acknowledging the truth of what Rustius had just said. Gone were the good old days of Augustus's rule. Rome lived in fear of the ambitious and bloodthirsty Sejanus, who was the de facto Emperor in Tiberius's absence, not that Tiberius was much better.

One of the legionnaires banged on the shutters of Marcellus's shop. "Open up, in the name of the Emperor," Rustius shouted.

Marcellus and Sylvia looked at each other in alarm. They didn't know what this was about, but they did know it wasn't good. Sylvia activated her electric defense, warning Marcellus not to touch her. Marcellus pulled up his shutters and was immediately seized by one of the legionnaires. Recognizing Sextus, he shouted, "Sextus, what's going on?"

Sextus looked down in shame. Rustius proclaimed loudly, "By order of the Emperor Tiberius, you and this woman are to come with us."

Marcellus saw Sylvia pulling out her gun. In great panic, he pointed to Sextus. "Antevorte, do not damage this one." The legionnaires looked at each other with a slightly confused look, thinking that perhaps Marcellus had lost his mind. He obviously was not properly understanding the situation, they believed.

Very mindful that she could not kill any of them, she fired at the legs of one of them, hoping beyond hope that she didn't hit the femoral artery. There was a loud bang. His leg erupted into blood. He screamed aloud and fell, clutching his wound. The three remaining legionnaires looked at her in amazement.

"I am the goddess Antevorte," she disdainfully said. "Am I required to punish another one of you?" They didn't know what to do. On the one hand, they didn't want to share their wounded comrade's fate. On the other hand, disobeying a command from Sejanus was very dangerous indeed.

Marcellus instantly understood their dilemma. He hoped to save his friend. "Sextus, we will be forced to leave. Tell your commander we were already gone."

"What about the one you wounded? How are we supposed to explain that?" sneered Rustius.

Marcellus looked at Sylvia for an answer. She replied, "Bring him to one of your doctors. There will be a small lead pellet deep in the wound. This must be extracted or he will die. It will give you a plausible excuse. You will say you heard a loud bang as you were walking away from this deserted shop and then this man fell to the ground, wounded. You will say you don't know what happened. It will be mysterious to all and though no one will be able to explain it, you will have successfully diverted attention from the failed arrest. *I'm not really sure if this will help them but I need them to buy it so that they'll let us go.*

Sextus looked at the others. They all nodded their agreement. Sextus gave Marcellus a look of profound gratitude. *This is the commander I remember,* he thought.

"What about Marcipor?" Sylvia asked. "It won't be safe for him here. And it won't be safe for him to come with us." She looked at the soldiers and gave them a somewhat threatening look.

Marcipor had witnessed the whole event from a concealed position. He came out from his hiding place.   "Do not worry about me, goddess. I have many friends in the city and I know one of them will help me out." *She is indeed a goddess, and a powerful one,* he thought in amazement.

He turned to Marcellus. There were actually tears in his eyes. "Be safe, Marcellus. You are a good man." He then turned to Sylvia. "Keep him safe, goddess," was all he said.

Chapter 8

Rome 31 CE

Sejanus was fuming as he was pacing back-and-forth. He was unused to not having his orders carried out. "So, am I to understand these two were not arrested?"

The Tribune was shaking. "No, Lord. They were not present at the wine shop when the soldiers arrived. I have been assured that our men searched the place thoroughly. It appeared deserted, as if they had left in a hurry."

Sejanus stopped pacing. "So, they must've had foreknowledge of their arrest?" he said, in a dangerously calm voice.

"It would appear so," the Tribune nervously answered.

"Which would lead me to believe there must be a spy among your men."

"That is a logical conclusion," the Tribune glumly replied.

"My next conclusion has to be you do not have proper control of your charges."

"But, Lord-"

"Are you about to offer an excuse? Do I accept excuses?"

"No, Caesar, but-"

"And now you're calling me Caesar. Are you not aware that Caesar is presently on the Isle of Capri? I do not know what I should do with you, Quintilius. I am very displeased. I shall have to think on this."

Quintilius gulped. This wouldn't be good. Sejanus had a certain reputation on how he dealt with those with whom he was displeased. He glumly allowed his imagination to go over the grim possibilities.

Sejanus moved on to a different topic. "I have heard that one of the arresting legionnaires was mysteriously wounded."

"That is so, ummm, Lord."

"I have also heard that a lead pellet was later removed from this man's wound by our doctor."

"That is also so, Lord."

"Finally, his wound was accompanied by a loud bang."

"All true, your highness."

"Hmmmm, you may go, Quintilius. I will deal with you later."

Sejanus grew deeply thoughtful. *Of course, his men sent to do the arrest were lying. The two we sought were probably there when his men arrived. Somehow, they were attacked by a new kind of weapon which scared them enough to allow their attackers to leave. This new weapon is much more important than any kind of glass. I must have this weapon. But first, I must talk to one of the soldiers who was actually there.*

An hour later found one of the soldiers trembling in front of Sejanus.

"Your name is Flavius, I believe."

"Yes, Caesar," Flavius quavered.

"Why is everyone insisting on calling me Caesar. The Emperor is Tiberius, not me." He paused briefly. "Anyway, Flavius, you were there when your comrade was wounded, is that not so?"

"Yes, your highness."

"And so were Marcellus and this unknown woman, is that not also so?"

Flavius started to protest but Sejanus interrupted him. "Do not lie to me, Flavius. If you speak truthfully, I promise you will not be in any trouble. But if you dare lie to me, your death will be most unpleasant. Am I understood?"

Flavius was pretty sure he was going to die anyway. A disobeyed order was a serious offense in ancient Rome, but he preferred a quick death to the one Sejanus threatened.

"Yes, they were there, highness. But it was the goddess-"

"Goddess?"

"Yes, highness. The lady with Marcellus was a goddess. I think she called herself Antevorte. She wounded one of us with her magic. I believe it was meant as a display. I am quite certain she could have killed us all. Attempting to arrest them would've been futile, resulting only in our deaths."

"So, you do not obey any command that might be dangerous to you. Is that what I'm to understand?"

"No, your highness," he unhappily replied, knowing his fate was sealed.

"Thank you, Flavius. You may go." After he left, Sejanus recalled his Tribune. "See that all four are executed, but make their deaths quick. Also, see if they have spoken to any about this incident. If they have, those spoken to should also be executed. We must keep this incident quiet. And we must find these two."

Later, Sejanus summoned one of his scribes, who specialized in religion. Not wasting any time, he brusquely asked, "Is there a goddess called Antevorte?"

The scribe paused a moment in thought. "Yes, Caesar," which just caused Sejanus to sigh. "Antevorte is the goddess of the future."

"Goddess of the future, hmmm? Thank you. You may go."

Goddess of the future. Goddess of the future. Well, goddess of the future, let's see what kind of future you have now, if you are indeed a goddess.

Chapter 9

Somewhere outside of Rome   31 CE

I knew I should've left this era earlier. But then again, Marcellus would still have been arrested, and all because of me. Christ, I can't desert him now.

They had left hurriedly, but not before Marcellus had gathered all the money he had saved, quite a few denarii and aurii.

"I think we need to get far away, perhaps-" he stopped, as he noticed Sylvia was fighting tears. "What is the matter, Antevorte?"

She tried unsuccessfully to stop the tears. "This is all my fault. I have completely disrupted your life, and now your very existence is threatened, all because of me."

"This never bothered you before," he commented with a slight edge.

He was shocked to see her start sobbing.

"Antevorte, I am sorry. That was most unkind." He took a chance and gently rubbed her arm up and down. "It is not your fault that a bloodthirsty tyrant rules in Rome. Your search should not have engendered any kind of danger, but the times are such now that one can lose his life at any time for any stupid reason."

She nodded, and seemed to pull herself together, as she wiped away some tears.

He was completely flummoxed. *So, she does have feelings.* He thought some more. *Was her haughtiness and coldness all just an act then? She may be a goddess, but she is also a woman.*

Seeking to distract her, he said, "Think of all the benefits I have gained. I had never been cleaner in my life. I have learned to be shy in performing my duties in the toilet. And I probably know the streets of Rome better now than I ever have."

She smiled gently at him. She knew what he was doing. *Such a kind, gentle man,* she thought.

He continued, "I know of a coupana about an hour down this road where we can find some sustenance and spend the night. I think our ultimate goal should be Gaul (modern-day France). We will never be safe in Italy."

They were currently on the Via Aurelia which ran north along the eastern coast of Italy and eventually connected to the Via Postumia. This road led into Gaul. The Roman roads were a marvel of engineering. They contained five separate layers of sand, crushed rock and concrete, all ending in a smooth curved top (for drainage) with cemented-in flat stones. Some of these roads survive even today and may appear bumpy now because the cement around the stones has been worn away.   The surface was smooth in Roman times. The Romans constructed 250,000 miles of these roads, of which 80,000 were paved, radiating throughout their empire.

They arrived at the coupana early that evening. Coupanas were somewhat like our modern inns, the main difference being they usually only offered one room for overnight stays. They also offered a variety of foods and wine for the weary traveler.

Sylvia and Marcellus said little to each other as they dined on some lamb, vegetables and wine. They both seemed lost in their thoughts and even avoided looking at each other. The owner, clearly impressed with Sylvia's looks, came over and tried to make some small talk. He smiled at Sylvia and addressed Marcellus, "Your wife is very beautiful, sir."

Marcellus looked over at Sylvia who gave a slight, almost imperceptible nod, indicating that he should go along with this pretense. "I thank you, sir," he answered simply.

"So, you two are from Rome?"

"Yes," Marcellus answered.

"My name is Varo, the owner of this poor establishment, and you are?"

Again, Sylvia gave him an imperceptible nod. "I am Marcellus and this is my wife, Aventia." He was careful not to use her real name even though he doubted Varo would be familiar with the minor goddess, Antevorte.

"And where might you two be headed?"

Marcellus was starting to get a bit annoyed with this man's nosiness. "We are on vacation, sir. We have no particular destination in mind, just thought we would enjoy the countryside and some views of the ocean." He had no intention of telling this man where they were really headed as he might be interrogated later on by agents of Sejanus.

Before Varo could come up with another question, Marcellus said, "We would like to stay overnight. Is your room available?"

Varo had the nerve to actually wink at Marcellus. "Yes, of course."

Marcellus, even more annoyed because of the wink, asked with a bit of an edge, "And what is the rate for the room?"

"Just one denarius."

That was an outrageous price but they were in no situation to be fussy.

They finished their meal and went upstairs to their room. There was only one bed in the room.

Both colored a bit as they looked at each other. "I shall sleep just outside your door," Marcellus announced, clearly embarrassed.

"And you don't think that won't look a little bit suspicious as you're supposed to be my husband and all?" She answered with an ironic look.

"Yes, stupid of me. I'll just sleep inside the door."

She looked at him and sighed. "No, Marcellus. You will sleep in the bed with me." *This is inevitable. I'm tired of fighting it.*

He was utterly astonished at her pronouncement and was silent for a moment. Then, completely embarrassed, he stammered, "That is not really a good idea, Antevorte. I will not be able to, ummm-“ He colored even more deeply. “The thing is, I am a man and you are a beautiful woman, so I, ummm, might be made uncomfortable.”

She couldn't help laughing. Even more embarrassed and a bit annoyed by her laughter, he added, “I might make you uncomfortable too,” which made her laugh even more.

The damage is already done. I'm not going to deny myself, or him, anymore. “I am very well aware of what will happen, Marcellus.” She smiled and patted the bed next to her. “Come,” she said, and started to remove her tunic.

Marcellus gasped at her beauty which was even more than his imagination had allowed. He stared briefly at her panties, the like of which he had never seen before. They were not cotton or linen. They were silky and seemed to be fastened by some strange, stretchy material. They snuggly outlined her perfect ass which went well with her perfect breasts. Somehow, this only inflamed his burgeoning erection even more.

She was amused and excited also at his obvious response. “Are you going to stand there and stare all day?” She smiled impishly. “Or are you going to allow nature to take its course?”

Not surprisingly, they spent the next little while allowing nature to take its course. Downstairs, Varo only smiled at the racket they were making. *Lucky man,* he thought enviously.

Chapter 10

Rome 31 CE

Sylvia woke up early the next morning, turned away from Marcellus on the bed and stared at the opposite wall. *This was just a huge, fucking mistake,* she thought miserably. *What in God's name was I thinking? There's no future. I have to go back. So now, not only do I disrupt his professional life, but I screw with his personal one too.* There was no doubt in her mind. The first time had been rough and passionate and needy. But there had been a lot of affection and care the second time. She knew he was involved, at least a little bit. *And if truth be told, I'm a bit involved also.*

She turned and looked over her shoulder at him. He was awake and looking thoughtful. He snuggled up to her, getting into the spooning position. He reached over and started massaging one of her breasts with his large hand. And then he started rocking slightly so that she could feel her bottom being erotically rubbed with his throbbing erection.

She groaned, thinking, *Who knew some of these Romans could be such good lovers.* It just felt so damn good.

He leaned forward and whispered into her ear, "Now you need to tell me who you really are. I know you are no goddess, Antevorte, or whatever your name really is. I have seen you using what I assume must be a weapon twice now. The weapon was not a magic instrument appearing from midair, as I saw you removing it from your toga last night when you were disrobing. It is no magical power; it is a weapon, a weapon the likes of which I've never seen, but a weapon just the same."

She stiffened, and tried to rise, but he held her firmly. "You should know, Antevorte, that I would never hurt you, but I need to know the truth." He continued massaging her breast and rubbing her bottom. And then he moved his other hand between her legs to her hotspot.

She groaned again. She couldn't believe the impossible situation she found herself in. On the one hand, she needed him. She wanted him inside of her, NOW. On the other hand, she needed to get up and get the hell out of here, but this latter desire was rapidly waning.

He kept up his seduction, but never made any further move to consummate the experience. She moaned and groaned, and tried to turn around to finish what he had started. There was no longer any thought of stopping. But he was being obstinate. "The truth, Antevorte. I want the truth."

She resisted saying anything with all her will power, but it was completely futile. She struggled with all her might but reason was slowly fading. She finally gave in, deciding, rightly or wrongly, there would be little harm in him knowing the truth. "Sylvia," she gasped. "My name is Sylvia, and I'm from the future, you bastard!"

Marcellus just smiled. "I will need more information… Sylvia… when we are finished, but for now," he turned her around. "We need to finish some more important matters." She just groaned.

She was absolutely furious with him when they were done. "I hope you're pleased with yourself. I never would've imagined you could be such a bastard. And this knowledge you've extorted from me is not going to do you any good."

"Extortion, huh? I would not have called it that. You sounded like you were having a pretty good time for someone who was being extorted. And now perhaps you can tell me what you meant when you said you come from the future."

She got up from the bed and started dressing, still thoroughly angry with him. "I'm pretty sure you're going to find a lot of this hard to believe."

"Maybe you should let me be the judge of that."

"To start, I'm from 2,000 years in the future, from a continent that your people don't even know exists."

He mused, *I saw her weapon at work. It appeared like magic to me. It's not that hard to believe she's from so far in the future. And why would she lie about something like that. But we are aware of the country called China.*

"If you're talking about China, we know about China."

"I'm not talking about China. If you sail westward, out of the Mediterranean, past Spain, onto the ocean there, you will need to travel over 4,500 miles (called *mille passum* in Roman times) to reach my land. And my land is as large as Europe as you know it."

"Incredible! The world is that large," he said, amazed.

"Not only is it that large, but it contains over seven billion people."

He was completely amazed but continued, "Tell me, ummm, Sylvia. Does the Roman Empire still exist?"

This dampened her anger. She looked up at him sadly. She knew this was probably important to him. "Well, firstly, the Empire split into two parts, Eastern and Western. I really don't know exactly when that happened. Your part of the Empire, the part with Rome as its capital, will fall a little over 400 years from now. And by then, Marcellus, Rome was scarcely more than a village, and the so-called Western Empire was an empire in name only."

He looked so morose that she added, "But the good news is the city of Rome still exists and has a population of close to 3 million people. It is now the capital of the country called Italy. People from the city of Rome now usually call themselves Italians rather than Romans."

"Tell me more about your time, Sylvia. I can hardly imagine what the world would be like 2,000 years from now."

"If Sejanus is after us, don't you think we better get going? Later on, rather than tell you, I think it would be better if I show you." She pulled out her mirror/computer. "I will be able to do that with this. You've already seen what it can do. But for now, I really think we should get going."

"You're right, of course." He looked at the mirror doubtfully. *Well anyway, she's a passionate woman.* He grinned to himself. *I think I know exactly how to get more truth out of her, mirror or no mirror.*

They both hurriedly finished dressing and went downstairs. Marcellus asked the owner, "Do you know where I can buy some horses?"

He answered, "There's a horse farm about 20 miles up this road. You should be able to get a couple there."

Before the owner could comment further, Sylvia urgently whispered into his ear, "Marcellus, I don't know how to ride horses." Unknown to both of them, she would have had an even harder time than she would in the present, as the Romans had not invented the stirrup.

"Thank you, sir, for your hospitality. We will be leaving now." Varo watched them leave and sighed, knowing he would miss the sight of her beauty.

Once outside, Marcellus asked her, "You really don't know how to ride a horse? Do they not have horses in your time?"

Annoyed at his tone, she petulantly answered, "Yes we have horses. But most of us don't use them. We have self-moving vehicles for traveling. I'll show you later."

"No problem. You'll ride on the horse with me." He thought a bit more about it. "Though that might create a different kind of problem," he added, smiling ruefully at her.

~~~~~~

Sejanus was pacing back-and-forth. He couldn't understand what the difficulty was. What had initially been a simple problem, had proved to be worrisome. It appeared there was a new and powerful weapon in his kingdom and he had not yet been able to secure it. He had sent out the message through his lighted semaphores to all garrisons on all the roads leading from Rome. "Be on lookout. Traveling duo. Tall, redheaded woman. Detain. Do not kill."

Thank goodness that woman is so tall, and redheaded to boot. Otherwise, this would've been an impossible task. Jupiter knows how many people traveled the Via Apia alone, never mind the rest of the roads radiating out of Rome, he glumly thought.
~~~~~~

The next day, his Tribune came in with some promising news. "We think we have located the couple traveling on the Via Aurelia. They stopped at a coupana yesterday and stayed overnight. The owner says the man's name was Marcellus. He was somewhat confused with the woman's name. He said Marcellus sometimes called her Antevorte, and other times Sylvia."

Sejanus waved his hand in dismissal. "I'm pretty sure Antevorte is not a goddess. She is pretending to be a goddess. We can assume her real name is Sylvia. Were they traveling by foot or on a horse?"

"They were on foot, highness."

"That's good, although they might try to acquire horses. In any event, even if they had horses, they could not have traveled further than Cosa. Have the garrison there arrest them."

Rutilius was the commander of the garrison at Cosa. For hours, his scouts had not turned up the two. There had been numerous false alarms and Rutilius was becoming seriously annoyed. *I don't know what so difficult about my orders. I have to keep repeating that the female is tall, with red hair. They keep coming back with erroneous reports. Red hair, for Jupiter's sake! Not brunette. Not blonde. Are these men not capable of looking above a woman's breast to see what color of hair she has! This is a waste of time and resources,* he thought. *What could be so important about these two? Still, what Sejanus orders is what I will do.*

Finally, a promising report came in. A tall lady with red hair along with a man. But they were not walking. They were riding together on a single horse. *Did they not have enough money for two?* thought an amused Rutilius. *I think I'll accompany the arresting detail. I want to see this for myself.*

Indeed, Sylvia and Marcellus were riding together most uncomfortably on a single horse. She was uncomfortable because of the horse. He was uncomfortable because of Sylvia. Regardless of the reasons, they were both pretty miserable.

"I can't believe your people don't ride horses," complained Marcellus.

She snapped back at him, "Why would we ride horses, when we can travel much more comfortably in a car that routinely travels 70 miles an hour?"

"Yes, well I'm really going to pay for this tonight," he ruefully answered. *A car? What in Jupiter's name is a car?*

She couldn't help giggling a bit. She knew all about blue balls, and he was providing ample evidence that he would indeed suffer tonight.

"I'm glad you find it funny. But I don't think you'll find it so funny when I am unable to perform."

She just grinned. *Based on what I've seen so far, my hunky Roman, I have little doubt that you will be unable to perform tonight. We may be on the run, but at least there's that.*

Just then, he noticed a detail of five or six soldiers on horses fifty or sixty yards away from them, coming on fast and with clear intent.

"Marcellus, hurry. Put me down. And once again, don't touch me." She activated her electric defense and pulled out her gun. Marcellus also dismounted. "Stay behind me, Marcellus," she warned. "And once again, don't touch me until I tell you it's safe."

The horsemen halted about 15 yards away. They dismounted and then fanned out in a semicircle so as to prevent any escape. Rutilius stepped forward. "By order of the Emperor Tiberius, I am placing you under arrest."

"You mean Sejanus, don't you," sneered Marcellus.

Before he could respond, Sylvia shouted out, "I am the goddess, Antevorte. I do not wish to harm you or your men, but you must withdraw while you have the chance."

Rutilius smiled. "Well you certainly are beautiful, my lady, but I don't know about the goddess part. I think maybe you are suffering from an overbearing ego problem." He turned to his men. "Arrest these two. Be careful not to harm them any more than necessary."

The men advanced. Two loud bangs split the air. Two of the legionnaires fell, clutching their legs in agony. The remaining men stopped in shock, and looked at their wounded comrades. "Commander, tell your men to withdraw. I do not wish to harm any more of them," Sylvia urged.

"Halt!" He ordered. He studied her carefully. He knew his men would think she had used magic on them. They would believe she was indeed a goddess. But Rutilius was a very intelligent, well-read man. He knew a weapon when he saw one. *So that's why Sejanus wants these two in custody. He wants to secure this amazing weapon. I probably could take her down with a well-aimed arrow, but Sejanus wants her alive.* He considered some more. *She has placed this man behind her. She is concerned for his safety. That is obvious. I would not be terribly surprised if they were even lovers. I think I know how I can take them.*

"Your magic is too powerful for us to overcome, goddess," he dissembled. "You may pass. Please do not harm any more of my men."

That was too easy, she thought. She deactivated her electric defense and they mounted the horse and passed by the soldiers, who were regarding them fearfully.

"This is a lost cause, Sylvia," Marcellus said despondently. They know who we are. They know where we are. It is just a matter of time."

Sylvia shared his mood. "I agree. I don't understand why we aren't already dead."

"I think they must've been ordered to take us alive. Sejanus probably wants to interrogate you about your weapon. It's obvious he's figured things out. Even that commander. Did you notice he did not show the same amount of fear and respect his men did? He's probably figured things out too."

He sighed. "Your people in the future have underestimated us. They think us more superstitious than what many of us actually are. We are not savages, Sylvia. We are civilized people capable of reasoning just like your people are."

"Yes, I can see that," she said simply. *He's right. We did think they would be more superstitious and prone to believing I'm a goddess. In their own way, they're as rational as we are. They're probably a step up from what society will be like in a thousand years.*

Rutilius ordered his scouts to follow them at a respectful distance. *They have to sleep sometime,* he thought.

A few hours later, Sylvia and Marcellus decided to camp for the night. They elected to take turns on guard duty, knowing full well they were being followed and observed.

"You have your orders, Decanus. Wait for the so-called goddess to be sleeping. It is very important that you make sure she is sleeping."

The agreed-upon time arrived. Sylvia was in a dead sleep. Marcellus looked over at her and shook his head. He doubted he'd be able to sleep so fitfully after what had transpired today. Suddenly, a hand was clamped over his mouth and two other soldiers grabbed his arms. Rutlius pulled out his knife and held it to Marcellus's throat.

"Goddess," he called out. Then in a louder voice, "Goddess, wake up!"

She startled awake. "One wrong move, Goddess, and this man is dead." This was a complete bluff. He had been ordered to take the two of them alive. "Now take out that amazing weapon of yours slowly and hand it over to me."

She hesitated. She knew she should kill them all, timeline be damned, but she couldn't bear the thought of Marcellus being killed. On the other hand, she could not allow the technology of this weapon being released in this time. Thank God Tegar had provided a solution. The Romans knew nothing about fingerprints. *Let's see them try to fire this weapon without my thumbprint,* she thought smugly.

Rutilius did not miss her smug expression. He knew she had something up her sleeve and he didn't like it at all. But his orders were to arrest them and deliver them to Sejanus. Anything else was not his responsibility. He figured they eventually would be killed. He looked at the beautiful Sylvia. *What a waste!* is all he thought.

Chapter 11

Rome 31 CE

Sylvia was dead tired. Her wrists, angry red where the tight ropes chafed, were killing her. She was being dragged by her bound wrists back to Rome, as was Marcellus. She was stumbling more than walking. Her captors weren't walking. They were on horseback. In fact, she and Marcellus were the only ones not on horseback. Their pace, though not too fast, was steady, to the point where she felt she must soon pass out. Rutilius had been instructed to punish them, without whipping or maiming. He figured this slow, steady, brutal pace would accomplish that.

She finally stumbled and fell. His decanus ran forward to whip her, standard practice with this process. "STOP!" Rucilius shouted. "She is not to be whipped." He looked down at her. "On your feet, my lady," he commanded.

She continued to sit, glaring up at him.

"Up, up, up," he commanded again.

She sneered back at him hoarsely, "Kill me now, if you must. I will not take another step."

Rutilius pondered his dilemma. He had been ordered not to physically harm her, merely to punish. So, what was he to do now? "My lady, if you do not rise now, I shall be forced to whip your man." This was a complete bluff as his orders from Sejanus included Marcellus.

Unaware of these orders, Sylvia tried to rise, but her knees buckled, and she fell again. She gave a panicked look, and tried again, with the same result. Tears started to form as she believed Marcellus would pay for her inability to get up.

Rutilius was not really a cruel man. He realized the situation and ordered, "Enough. We shall make camp here." He ordered one of his men to help Sylvia.

An hour later, Marcellus and Sylvia were securely bound to a tree by their ankles. A promise not to attempt to untie their constraints won them the luxury of not having their hands secured. Also, Rutilius assured them a guard would be watching them the entire time. Any attempt at escape would result in both hands and feet being securely bound.

Sylvia was sleeping, dead to the world, when Rutilius approached Marcellus. "You were a soldier, weren't you Marcellus?"

"Yes I was. I fought in the German campaigns."

"I thought so. The way you carry yourself, and the fact you are not nearly as tired as the woman. You obviously are accustomed to marching." He paused and then continued, "I wonder why Sejanus is so interested in you?"

"Hah! I'm pretty sure we both know. He wants to get his hands on Sylvia's weapon."

"Where did she get it anyway? Where is she from?"

"If I told you, you wouldn't believe me."

"Try me."

"Well, she first tried to pass herself off as the goddess Antevorte."

"What!? I know she's beautiful but isn't that a little much?"

"Not as far-fetched as you might think. She literally appeared out of thin air. One minute, my shop was empty except for my slave. The next minute, this beautiful woman appeared, claiming to be a goddess. She tried to pass this off by acting pretty haughty, giving out commands like she expected to be obeyed. I didn't like her too much at first. But the haughtiness turned out to be an act. She's actually quite kind."

Rutilius interrupted, "Out of thin air! Come on." Rutilius was another one who really didn't believe in gods or goddesses.

"I told you, you would find it hard to believe. But that is what happened.
You can choose to believe it or not. I really don't care."

"Sorry. Continue on with your story."

"I'm sure many would've remained convinced she was a goddess,
especially after she used her weapon on a soldier who tried to accost her.
It would've seemed like magic to many. But quite frankly, I never believed
in the gods and goddesses. After a while, I came to realize she was no
goddess, but a person who possessed advanced weaponry. I eventually
got the truth out of her."

"And?"

"She claimed to be from the future, 2,000 years in the future, to be precise."
He looked at Rutilius to gauge his reaction.

"Do you believe her?" The commander dubiously asked.

"Yes I do, and I'll tell you why. That weapon of hers is way beyond our
capability to build. She also has a personal defense system that can
prevent anyone from touching her if she so desires. Again, this is more
advanced than what we are capable of producing."

"Then why did she come here? Did she want to set herself up as some
sort of queen?"

"No. This is the funny part. She is here to procure a formula for creating
bendable, unbreakable glass. Someone here has invented this process
and that's why Sejanus was so interested in us at first. Apparently, that
doesn't exist in the future and it would be worth a lot of money for someone
to start producing it there."

"You're joking! She's here to make money? Only that?"

"Yes. But not for her. For her boss. A man named Tegar."

"I guess that shouldn't be too surprising. Money is the cause of much evil
here too," Rutilius mused ruefully. Then, changing the subject, he

observed, "You two are lovers. I've seen the way you look at each other. There is no doubt."

Marcellus colored slightly and then admitted, "Yes, we are."

Rutilius smiled. "I can't say I blame you. She is truly a beautiful woman."

Marcellus sighed. "Yes she is. And I cannot deny that is part of the reason I am in love with her, but it's not the only reason. She is brave and very self-confident. And that's not all. I have never met a woman who acts the way she does. She doesn't act subservient to me. And she doesn't try to use the so-called womanly guiles to get what she wants. Instead, she considers herself my equal. She acts like a man would towards me. At first, this flustered me, but now I like it. We are equals in this relationship, each bringing our own strengths to it. In fact, the only time I have ever seen her behave like a so-called woman is when she shed tears over the harm she believed she had caused to me by coming here."

Both men were silent and thoughtful for a while. Rutilius finally said, "I like you, Marcellus. I wish I didn't have to deliver the two of you to Sejanus. I know what a bastard that guy has been. I know what is probably going to happen to the two of you. But orders are orders. I have no choice in this matter."

"I don't like it either, commander, but I understand. And, from one soldier to another, I appreciate you saying this to me."

Chapter 12

Rome 31 CE

Lucius Aelius Sejanus was born in 20 BC to the equestrian class. Coming from this class, he did not have access to the higher levels of power. This did not stop the overly ambitious Sejanus. By 15 CE he had become the prefect of the Imperial bodyguard called the Praetorian Guards. He achieved real power by winning the undying love of the 12,000 men in the Praetorian Guards. He further consolidated his power by becoming a close confidant of the Emperor Tiberius. In 26 CE Tiberius retired to the Isle of Capri, never really wanting the duties and responsibilities of being Emperor. He turned these over to Sejanus who resided in Rome and became the de facto Emperor. Sejanus used his position to remove all those whom he saw as impediments to his eventual climb to the throne, thus initiating a reign of terror. Therefore, it should not be too surprising that Sylvia and Marcellus were both terrified at being arrested by him. This usually meant a death sentence. But Sylvia had a plan.

In a show of unprecedented kindness, Marcellus and Sylvia were imprisoned together in a fairly nice room, instead of the dungeon they expected. Sylvia believed quite correctly that Sejanus was trying to stay on her good side so that she would eventually demonstrate how to use the gun he had procured. Marcellus, on the other hand, had no idea but was very distrustful on how long this good fortune would last.

"You promised to show me some of your world," he said after their lovemaking. "Now would be as good a time as ever."

She gave him an impish grin. "So, I was not enough to satisfy you? You require further stimulation?"

He laughed. "Don't get me started, woman. You know you're already wearing me out."

She sighed. "Then all the rumors I've heard about Roman men are not true, I guess."

"I know what you're trying to do, Sylvia, and it won't work. Not now, anyway. For now, I wish to learn more of your world. We'll deal with other matters a little later." He gave her a look that curled her toes.

"Well, if you insist." She retrieved her mirror/computer and gave it the command to activate. "You've heard me talk about not having the need for horses. Look here now." She showed him a typical New York City traffic scene, then followed it with a scene from Formula One."

She was telling the truth, he thought in amazement. *This mirror is a wondrous invention.* Marcellus spent many minutes, as was his habit, studying the moving pictures. He seemed more impressed with the racing scene. "How fast were those vehicles going?" He asked.

"A little over 200 mph. Remember when I explained miles per hour? The number of miles traveled by a vehicle in an hour."

"That astonishes me. I would not even have believed a human being could survive traveling such speeds."

Next, she showed him a jet taking off and one landing. She didn't say anything, just looked at him in amusement for his reaction.

He gasped. "These are boats that are flying, are they not? And they carry people, do they not?"

"Yes, and they are going over 600 mph at 35,000 feet."

He asked her to show him this scene over and over again for the next 10 minutes or so. He was amazed, yes, but he was enjoying the scene also. *That we have come so far,* he thought in wonder.

Finally, he just shook his head. "We must seem very primitive to you."

"Not at all. Your world is fascinating and a much better world than will exist a thousand years from now. Your baths, your engineering, and a lot of your technology will be lost as Europe descends into a dark age which lasted for almost a thousand years. The only real advancements made will be in warfare. It is only in the last 500 years or so before my time, in the period that started with something we call the Renaissance, did my world emerge and become possible."

He pondered this for a moment. It was all so much to take in. "Show me more," he enthusiastically demanded.

She looked at him coyly. "Maybe later. There is a price to pay for these revelations, you know. Something you called 'other matters.' I think it is time for me to collect."

And she did.

The next day, she was brought before Sejanus. He looked her over, head to toe, clearly admiring what he was seeing. "You truly are a beautiful woman, Antevorte." He hesitated, then, "No, I don't really like that name. I think I shall call you… Let's see… Sylvia. That seems more appropriate," he said sarcastically.

His whole manner changed. He produced the gun he had in his possession. "Show me how this confounded thing works," he demanded. "All it does for me is make a clicking noise when I press this button."

He looked at her menacingly and warned, "I don't suppose you would be stupid enough to try using this on me. I have no doubt you realize what would happen to Marcellus."

Thank God this gun is thumbprint controlled. I am the only one who can fire it, unless they cut off my thumb. I don't think I have to worry about that as they have no idea why it won't fire. I do have to make up a story to explain why it won't work for him, she thought.

"This weapon will only work if you're a god or goddess," she explained.

"STOP THIS NONSENSE!" He roared. "I know you are not a goddess."

His vehemence frightened her. He advanced on her menacingly. She briefly considered turning on her electric defense, but then decided not to. She figured he might execute her, once recovered, if she shocked him. In any event, she knew she would not be able to wear this tunic much longer, as it was starting to show its age. She figured she'd better learn how to use her wits instead of physical force to get herself out of tight spots.

He wrapped one arm around her waist and clamped his other hand on her breast. "I think I know a way I can prove you're not a goddess," he sneered.

She tried to push him away to no avail. "So the great Sejanus is now going to rape me," she jeered.

Surprisingly, her rebuke worked. He released her, and then barked, "Just show me how the fucking thing works then."

His show of aggression and obvious willingness to use physical violence had frightened her. "You may not believe me to be a goddess, but I assure you, I am the only one able to use this weapon. It is the way it has been designed in case it fell into the hands of an enemy." She tried to hide the quaver in her voice but failed.

From long experience with interrogations, Sejanus knew she was telling the truth. "So, if no one other than you can use this weapon, what use are you to me then? I simply no longer have any reason to keep you two alive." He laughed. "Unless you want to join one of my Legions."

But Sylvia had a plan. She had prepared for just this contingency. "You are correct, Sejanus. I am not a goddess. But do you know where I come from?"

"Does it matter?" He snarled.

"Yes it matters, Sejanus, because I can be of use to you."

"Go on," he said, mildly interested.

"I am from the future, 2,000 years in the future to be precise."

"Such nonsense," he scoffed. "And even if it were true, how is this useful to me?"

"Think, Sejanus. Would it not be advantageous for you to know what your enemies are going to do tomorrow, next week, or even next month? Or would it not be useful to learn which course of action will work, and which won't?"

He grew thoughtful and then derided her. "But you're not from the future, are you? You might be delusional, but that's about it."

"Oh, no?" She sarcastically scoffed. "Then how do I know you are Drusus's widow, Livilla's lover? And how do I know you plan to ask Tiberius for permission to marry her? He's going to refuse by the way. He's going to suggest you marry her daughter, Helen."

His eyes widened. How could she possibly know this? True, she hadn't realized this had already happened. But no one except he and Tiberius had been privy to this conversation. Even the slaves had been dismissed from the room.

She recognized victory when she saw it. "I will help you, Sejanus, but I have conditions."

"You are hardly in a position to make demands," he sneered.

"Nonetheless, I have them. No physical harm will come to Marcellus or me. We will no longer be locked in our room. We consent to being accompanied by a guard or as many guards as you desire, whenever we leave our room or this palace. If these conditions are met, I will be at your service."

Sejanus didn't like this, but he could see the great advantage it would give him. "I agree. It will be so. But if you or Marcellus attempt to escape, he will be put to death, and information will henceforth be tortured out of you. I hope you understand."

"I do," she gulped. *Thank god he doesn't have long to live,* she thought, before leaving the room.

Chapter 13

Rome 31 CE

A few weeks passed and Sylvia was feeling tremendously guilty. How many deaths had she been responsible for? She had taken great care to consult her computer and determine which of her victims had actually died in Sejanus's treason trials without her revelations. This should have helped, but it didn't.

Marcellus was all too aware of the increasing depression suffered by his lover. "Surely you cannot blame yourself for deaths that would've occurred anyway without your intervention?"

"I realize that's how I should feel. It's not rational to feel bad about this. And that is what my logical mind is telling me. Unfortunately, this is not how I *feel* about this. Have you ever contributed to someone's unjust death? Believe me, it's not an easy thing to bear. Do you understand me, Marcellus? My mind says I'm not responsible. My heart says I am."

Marcellus just sighed. He knew Sylvia was a good person. He knew she was doing what was needed for them to survive, but he hated to see her tearing herself apart over it.

"This is probably harder for you because you probably don't have monsters like Sejanus in your time."

She just laughed ruefully. "You have to be kidding, right? We have had much worse in my time. There are people like Hitler and Stalin who are responsible for millions of deaths. Human nature doesn't change with the passing of years, Marcellus. Most people are good. Some are monsters. The trick is to try to prevent the monsters from ever gaining a position of power."

He was a bit surprised. "I would've thought the march of civilization would've changed all that. It's disappointing, to say the least, to learn that we never learn."

She grinned sadly at him. "If you're trying to make me feel better, it's not working."

"Marcellus, I have another important matter to discuss with you." He had noticed her rummaging urgently in her pouch and at last giving up with a despairing look.

"I have a need for something, umm." She colored deeply.

He became concerned. "What is it, my love?"

"I did not expect to be here more than a month, you see. So, I did not properly prepare, umm, for my needs." She colored even more deeply.

 "What needs?"

She could not look at him. She looked away. "My womanly needs," she answered meekly.

Marcellus was being a bit thick. "Womanly needs?"

She looked at him in exasperation. "For Christ's sake, Marcellus, you know, what happens to a woman every month."

Marcellus knew better than to laugh but he had difficulty holding it in. Finally, when he trusted himself not to break into laughter, he asked, "How have you dealt with this the last little while?"

"We have different manufactured items that we use, depending on whether we are virgins are not," she answered, still clearly embarrassed. "Ummm, I have run out of this item. I need a substitute."

Still fighting laughter, he replied, "I don't think I'm the proper person to ask. I believe they use rags. I think you should ask one of the servant girls."

"For God's sake, Marcellus, don't you think I've already realized this? The problem is arousing suspicion with them that I would not already have such knowledge at my age. Will you try to find out for me?"

He no longer found this quite as funny. "I will try, Sylvia. But those women are going to find me really weird asking questions like this."

Serves you right for finding this funny, she thought cruelly.

A few days later Marcellus was walking towards his old shop with a guard following behind. He had failed to convince Sylvia to come with him. He had felt a little outside time would help with her depression. He finally arrived at the shop and was saddened to see it closed and looking deserted. He turned around to commiserate with the guard with whom he had become friendly the last little while. He was shocked to see the guard was not there. He had not noticed when the guard had been hailed by one of his former buddies, sitting at a café. The guard had stopped to talk with his friend briefly, figuring he could catch up to Marcellus if he didn't linger too long. Unfortunately, he did linger too long and when he turned back to the street, Marcellus was nowhere to be seen. As luck would have it, he did not know where Marcellus's shop was. He knew he would be in trouble. He would probably be whipped if he told the truth. So, he reported that Marcellus had escaped. He did not realize the consequences for Sylvia and Marcellus in so doing.

Marcellus was already in a panic as he tried to hurry back to Sejanus's palace, when he was accosted by three soldiers who had been sent to find him. He started to explain when one of them punched him in the mouth, knocking him to the ground, and leaving him groggy. The other two picked him up and bound his wrists. They then headed back to the palace with their prisoner in tow.

Sylvia was lying in her bed, feeling despondent, when the door burst open and two soldiers rushed in. They roughly picked her up from the bed and dragged her out.

"What- what's going on?" She squealed.

"You are under arrest by order of Sejanus," one of the soldiers barked.

She was half carried, half dragged to the dungeon, where she saw Marcellus was already chained by the ankle to the wall. He was showing signs of having been physically abused. They pushed her in but didn't chain her. She hurried to Marcellus. "Are you all right? What's going on?"

"They think I tried to escape. I was just going to see my shop. Somehow, my guard got distracted and I lost him." He looked at her glumly. "His fault, not mine, but I suppose to avoid punishment, he reported that I was trying to escape."

"Oh, no!" She gasped. "They will execute you if they think you tried to escape."

"I know," he unhappily answered.

The hours passed. She continually demanded to see Sejanus to no avail. Finally, a guard opened the cell door and entered. She started to head to the open door, thinking she was finally going to get an audience with Sejanus.

The guard laughed and roughly grabbed her. "Where do you think you're going, sweetheart? I was thinking I might put that wonderful body of yours to good use before it's damaged by Sejanus."

Oh God, she thought. *It's a damn good thing I was still wearing this tunic when they arrested me.* "Computer, activate defense," she said in English. The guard was shocked to the ground.

Marcellus had been straining against his chain. *I wish she had held on and killed him,* was his angry thought. He had already learned that death would result if Sylvia did not release her victim. Sylvia made no move to exit through the open cell door. Instead, she yelled for one of the other guards, who eventually appeared. The newer guard was surprised to see his comrade lying unconscious on the floor with the cell door open.

"Now can we finally see Sejanus," she fumed. "It should be pretty obvious that I had no intention of escaping. This man," she pointed to the inert guard, "tried to sexually accost me."

A couple of hours later, Sejanus did make an appearance. "So this is the other weapon you have that I've heard about."

"It is. But once again, I am the only one able to use it. This is not why I want to speak to you. Marcellus was not trying to escape. His guard was negligent in his duty. Marcellus did not notice that the guard was no longer behind him. He was arrested while he was making his way back here. I don't think you should be jumping to conclusions when a man's life is at stake," she angrily finished.

"And you should not be impertinent when speaking to your superiors," said Sejanus, clearly annoyed.

"You are not my superior," she calmly replied.

"You are brave, my lady, speaking thusly to a man who holds the power of life and death over you."

"While this is true, it still does not make you my superior. Anyway Sejanus, I do not wish to continue this argument. I wish to convince you of Marcellus's innocence. Will you grant me the grace of listening?"

Sejanus studied her and then turned to one of his guards. "Summon the guard who was assigned to Marcellus."

Marcellus himself witnessed the whole scene in admiration of Sylvia. *She's as brave as a tiger,* he mused.

Marcellus's guard came rushing in five minutes later. He was clearly worried. "You called for me, my lord?"

"I did. Marcellus claims he is innocent. He was not trying to escape. He maintains you were remiss in your duties. Now it is not surprising that a man who is about to be executed for his crimes would claim innocence, but we need to know if he is telling the truth."

The guard looked up in surprise. *He will be executed! I was not aware of this. How can I allow a man to be put to death because of my lie? Especially Marcellus, whom I have found to be a fine man. Yet I will be punished, probably severely, if I tell the truth. Yet I know I probably will not be able to live with myself if I allow this to happen. Fuck!*

He looked glumly at Sejanus and then straightened his shoulders. "Ummm, he is telling the truth, my Lord. I got distracted, but only for a moment. I know this is not an excuse. I would never have lied if I realized his penalty would be death. I thought he might be whipped, but not killed."

Sejanus frowned at the guard. He turned to the other guards. "This man is to be given 30 lashes, and he is to be demoted one rank." He then looked at Marcellus and Sylvia. He did not apologize. "Let this be a lesson to you two that I am dead serious in what will happen if you try to escape. Guard, release these two." He gazed disdainfully at them. "You may return to your room."

Thank God Marcellus's guard was ethical. It couldn't have been easy to tell the truth when he knew how severe Sejanus could be, thought Sylvia.

Whereas Marcellus's only thought was, *What an arrogant prick! Even if he lied, I liked that guard. Sextus probably never realized what would happen to me if I tried to escape.*

Their lovemaking that night was very intense as they both realized how close they had come to the end of everything.

Chapter 14

Rome 31 CE

Marcellus had an undying interest in Sylvia's world.

"You know, this is borderline pestering, with you after me all the time," she groused.

"If you could see 2,000 years into *your* future, wouldn't you be interested?" Marcellus responded.

She sighed again. "Point taken. You know I would. So, let's see. Oh, I know. You're going to like this." She called up a video of the Apollo 11 moon landing and activated Latin subtitles.

By this time, Marcellus understood that videos were some kind of theater. He was very impressed at the launch of the Saturn booster. "Is this a new weapon? It seems devastating."

She laughed. "Typical man. Not everything is a weapon you know. Keep watching."

There was a lot Marcellus didn't understand. Since Marcellus had never really understood television, she had to stop the video and tried again to explain broadcasting and how it could transmit from thousands of miles away. At the end, she still wasn't sure if he got it.

When he saw the astronauts floating in their capsule, he exclaimed, "Now you're tricking me. People cannot float. These are trick pictures you're showing me." He turned to her. "You have a funny sense of humor, Sylvia."

She laughed again. "If you're in outer space, you can float."

"Outer space?"

This time she sighed deeply. "The heavens. These men are in the heavens."

He still looked very skeptical. "Are you trying to convince me of this goddess bit again?"

"No. What makes you say that?"

"You said these men are in the heavens. How did they get there?"

"Remember in the beginning of the video, you asked me if this was a weapon. I said it wasn't. It is actually a vehicle. The men you saw floating were in the vehicle. It is this vehicle which carried them to the heavens. If you can hold your questions and just watch the whole video, a lot will be made apparent to you," she said exasperatedly.

He grumbled, "I will do so, but I still think you're trying to trick me, for some unknown reason."

Neil Armstrong finally stepped off the ladder onto the surface of the moon. Marcellus turned to Sylvia obviously awestruck as realization slowly sank in. "The moon," he almost whispered. "Is this true? Have these men traveled to the moon?

She nodded.

"Your world is marvelously wonderful, Sylvia."

"A lot of it is, Marcellus. But a lot of it isn't. Computer, show the first 30 minutes of *Saving Private Ryan.* Latin subtitles, please.*"

He watched the battle scene raptly. When it was over, he said to Sylvia, "You think I haven't seen such, my love? Sure, the means of destruction are different, but a battlefield is a battlefield. The main difference I saw here is that our killing is much more up close and personal. Your people use variations of your gun and other things I didn't quite understand. I was more impressed that your theater could seem so realistic, than what was going on. Like I said, I've already seen the like." He looked at her significantly. "Many times," he added.

This was a sobering thought. Sylvia tried to lighten the mood by showing a couple of sitcoms like *All in the Family,* and *Friends,* with Latin subtitles of course. This didn't work at all. The two cultures were simply too different for Marcellus to get most of the humor. "I'm sorry, love. I know this is supposed to be funny. I can hear the audience laughing, but I simply don't get it."

Finally, she got a brainstorm, and showed him the 1960s version of *Ben Hur*. He enjoyed it immensely and took great pleasure in pointing out the fallacies.

Later he admitted, "They got most things right, Sylvia. And I'm still amazed at how realistic your theater can be. I do have a question for you, however. Who is this Jesus Christ? Was he a real person?"

She started to explain, "Christ started one of the largest religions in the world, Christianity. It won't really catch on here for another two or three hundred years." Suddenly, she stopped. Her eyes grew wide. "Oh my god! Marcellus, he's still alive right now! He won't be crucified for another two years. He's in Palestine at this very moment."

"This theater, ummm, this *movie* seems to say this man was a god. You know I don't believe in gods or goddesses, Sylvia. Do the people of your time still believe in these things?"

"Some do, and some don't. It's all a question of faith. And I'm certainly not going to get into a religious debate with you. As a matter of fact, I can think of something much better we can do right now."

Her lascivious look was all it took to get him going again. And she turned out to be right, he did enjoy it much more than any religious debate.

The next day found Marcellus uncharacteristically morose. Sylvia was so in love with him that she picked up on his mood very quickly. "So my love, you're being a bit quiet today."

"I know, sweetheart. I know. It's that damn Sejanus. I know I don't have to tell you how dangerous he is. I came this close to being executed, and for what?" He asked exasperatedly. "One small misunderstanding, which wasn't even my fault. Not to mention that you would've been tortured. It's like walking on egg shells. You never know when that bastard is going to turn on us. He's just so fucking dangerous!"

Sylvia looked around to make sure no one was within earshot. She leaned in to him closely and quietly said, "We won't have to worry for too much longer. I don't know exactly when it happens. I wish I had studied the history of this period more closely. But Sejanus dies this year, of that I'm certain. He will be executed." In actuality, Sylvia could've looked up the exact date on her computer but she did not do so. She feared her actions helping Sejanus might've changed the timing slightly. She did not want Marcellus to act carelessly, thinking he knew the exact date. Better not to know exactly.

Marcellus's eyes widened. "Are you sure?" He asked very hopefully.

She looked at him dolefully. "Yes, I'm sure. You need to remember, Marcellus, that for me this is ancient history. It's already happened. It's in the history books."

"Yes, I guess sometimes I forget exactly where you're from."

Sylvia didn't know exactly when this event, for which they prayed, would happen, but the time was actually upon them. It was late October, 31 CE.

The Roman matriarch Antonia had discovered a plot against the Emperor Tiberius, led by the ambitious Sejanus who believed he was very close to becoming the next Emperor. Sejanus normally censored all correspondence to Tiberius but Antonia, the youngest daughter of Marc Antony, had been in the habit of sending Tiberius poetry which Sejanus no longer bothered checking. Among the scrolls of poetry, she hid a scroll detailing the plot against Tiberius.

Tiberius was in a quandary. Sejanus controlled and was very popular with the 12,000 men of the Praetorian Guard. They might not obey an order to arrest Sejanus. Such an order might even have the opposite effect, pushing forward the conspiracy out of expediency. Such was Tiberius's fear, that he made arrangements to flee Capri if things went sideways.

A strategy was developed. Sejanus's second-in-command, Macro, was promised leadership of the Praetorian Guard when Sejanus fell. He was then given two scrolls, one to read in the Senate. When the time came, Macro ordered all of the Praetorian Guard to their barracks outside the city. When questioned about this strange command, Macro showed them the first scroll, signed and sealed by Tiberius, to obey this command, which they did. Macro then put the Night Guard in charge, just outside of the Senate. The Night Guard felt no particular loyalty to Sejanus.

Sejanus finally made an appearance and asked Macro about the scroll he was still carrying as he had heard nothing about it from Tiberius. Macro said he was merely told to read it in the Senate, but he believed it was an announcement declaring that Sejanus was to be a tribune of the people. This greatly pleased Sejanus who was blissfully unaware of what was about to come down.

So great was the expectation of Sejanus, that some Roman historians maintain he did not understand he was being denounced as a traitor when the scroll was first read out. He was arrested by the Night Guard and dragged out of the Senate. When he looked about, and saw there was no Praetorian Guard to save him, he finally realized he was doomed. He was dragged to the City Prison. Not being very popular, he was jeered and struck by the passing crowd on the way.

The Senate passed the order of execution the following day and Sejanus was garroted and his body tossed in the Tiber River. The executions were not limited to him. His small children were also executed. His little girl asked what had she done wrong and promised to be good if they let her go. The Roman guards hesitated because they could not execute a virgin by law. One of them solved that problem in a grisly matter and she was then executed. Their mother subsequently committed suicide. The purges lasted for months. All those formerly allied with Sejanus were put to death. Not surprisingly, Tiberius had proved he could be as bloodthirsty as Sejanus.

Marcellus and Sylvia knew something was going on. There were the sounds of lots of people running about, followed by some screaming. Before they could even think of leaving, a soldier popped his head into their room, and growled, "Stay here, if you know what's good for you."

"It must be happening, Marcellus. The end of Sejanus. That soldier gave good advice. We should just hunker down here and hope for the best. You know, they even killed his family which included little children. Let's hope we're not seen as supporters of Sejanus. If we are, we're as good as dead. If memory serves me right, the purges went on for months."

It took a couple of days before anyone dealt with the two of them. By this time, they were in a pretty weakened condition. They had not eaten and were only able to drink the water that had already been in their room. Finally, a guard entered and bid them to follow. They were brought to Sejanus's throne room where a squat, powerfully-built man sat.

"I am Quintus Naevius Cordus Sutorius Macro, the new prefect of the Praetorian Guard." He looked them over carefully. "I really do not know who you are and why you are here. Though I suspect you are supporters of Sejanus."

Sylvia stepped forward before Marcellus could say a word. "I am Sylvia, and this is Marcellus," she said, pointing to Marcellus. "We have never been supporters of Sejanus. Any duties we performed for him were under duress. You merely have to ask the guards assigned to us to learn the truth of this."

"But you did perform duties for him," Macro pressed.

Sylvia knew she was fighting for their lives. "Under duress," she nearly shouted. "Our choice was to do this or die. Again, I implore you to check with our guards to see that I am speaking truth."

"I will do so." He addressed Marcellus. "I find it strange you allow this woman to speak for you. Why is this so?"

Marcellus frowned. "She may be a woman, but she is more powerful than me. It is her powers, not mine, that Sejanus coerced. I am alive only because this woman insisted that I live, before she used her powers in the service of Sejanus."

"This becomes more interesting by the minute. What 'powers' are you referring to?"

"That is something for the Emperor to hear and no one else," Sylvia haughtily answered.

"You are indeed brave, my lady, to speak so in front of one who holds the power of life and death over you."

Sylvia looked coolly at him. "If you should be unwise and put us to death and if the Emperor ever learns what power you denied him, I think your stay on this planet would be very short."

Macro considered if she was bluffing. *This woman has a funny way of speaking, but I'm unwilling to take the chance.* Having learned his lesson, Tiberius had spies watching Macro's every move. Macro figured he would rather be safe than sorry.

"Very well then. You both shall be transported to the Isle of Capri where the Emperor will decide your fate."

Chapter 15

Isle of Capri 31 CE

Sylvia and Marcellus once again found themselves confined to a well-endowed room, this time in Tiberius's palace. And what a palace it was! It made anything they had seen in Rome look like a peasant's hut. Marble everywhere. Statues everywhere. Indoor plumbing resulting in indoor baths and toilet facilities. It must have contained 40 or 50 rooms.

It had already been several days and they had not seen hide nor hair of Tiberius. They had not been allowed to leave their room. Meals were brought to them. Chamber pots were also provided and changed daily. Though they made good use of their time alone, their patience was coming to an end.

"So whose brilliant idea was it to have you appear as a goddess?" Marcellus asked.

"Where does this come from?"

"I'm just curious."

"I suppose, Tegar, although Chuck was opposed to it."

"Chuck was that other time traveler, right?"

"Yes."

"Well it seems he had more common sense than your Tegar. You don't look like a typical Roman at all. Tegar must've thought we're all superstitious buffoons." Marcellus thought a bit more. "Were you and Chuck lovers?"

Sylvia was surprised at the question. "Why? Are you jealous?"

"No," answered Marcellus, not too convincingly.

Sylvia decided to have a little fun at his expense. "Chuck is a very good-looking man, you know. He's taller than me, and very well built. And he's well-experienced in the romantic arena, and-"

"Enough! I get the point."

Sylvia just laughed. "Marcellus, I'm teasing you. Chuck is happily married. He was my instructor." She looked at his expression, and laughed again. "He was my instructor, in time traveling, and that's all. We didn't even like each other at first, but now we're friends. And anyway, my lover, how could anyone ever replace you."

This seemed to mollify him.

Finally, after a few more days, a guard came to see them.

"The Emperor wishes an audience with you. Come with me."

They were being led down a long hall when they noticed a young, blond man conversing with a couple of women in a somewhat opulent room they were passing.

"Oh my God," gasped Sylvia dumbstruck. "I think that's Caligula."

"Shhh, shhh," urged Marcellus. "He hates that name. Don't let him hear you say it."

"Isn't that his name?" she asked, somewhat surprised.

Marcellus was also surprised at her ignorance. "What kind of name would 'little boots' be? That's what Caligula means. Caligula was a nickname given to him by the soldiers in the German campaign when Gaius Julius Caesar Germanicus was a little boy. He's a fine young man and one can only hope he becomes Emperor after Tiberius passes."

Sylvia gaped at him. "Gaius Germanicus, or Caligula as he is known in my time, is *not* a fine young man. He does become Emperor and turns out to be a monster worse than Sejanus. He is finally killed by his own Praetorian Guard when they've had enough of his travesties. He only ruled for five years, if memory serves me right."

"That is very surprising. His father, Germanicus Julius Caesar, was a famous general who was expected to be the next Emperor after Augustus. He was very highly regarded by the Roman people. Somehow, Tiberius managed to prevent this and is suspected of having caused Germanicus's death," whispered Marcellus.

"So, Tiberius is not a nice man," Sylvia whispered back ironically. "Why am I not surprised."

"By the gods, no! Be very careful what you say to him or you might find yourself being thrown over the cliffs like so many others."

Marcellus looked at her somberly. "I worry about you, my love. Tiberius may be old, but the rumors are he's very depraved. You are a beautiful woman and that is why I worry."

"You need not worry about me. I am wearing my special tunic, and-"

"No, no, no, no! You cannot use that against the Emperor. That would guarantee your death!" Now Marcellus was really worried.

"I am not stupid, Marcellus. I have a plan that does not involve me shocking the Emperor."

Before entering the balcony where it seemed Tiberius preferred greeting guests, she activated the tunic's defense. She worried a bit about the specially designed tunic finally starting to show its age. Even the specially designed materials of its composition were ultimately subject to the ravages of time.

So this is Tiberius, mused Sylvia. *Looks like any old, decrepit man from our time.* The person in question was returning Sylvia's inspection, half lying on his lounge.

"You truly are a beautiful woman, madam, if a bit tall for my tastes." It was pretty obvious he was having lecherous thoughts about her, despite her height. *Even if I end up having to kill her, there's no reason I can't enjoy her beforehand*

Sylvia did not miss the type of inspection she was undergoing. *I guess a dirty old man is a dirty old man. They exist in all ages, but this one is entitled and has absolute power. I'd better be really careful.*

"I thank you for the compliment, Caesar," she said, forcing a smile. *And I'd rather be tossed in a vat of acid before I let you touch me.*

"Yet, I can't for the life of me understand why Sejanus kept you and your lover alive. Or should I say, husband? Which is it, by the way?"

Sylvia colored. How could she answer that question? "I am a goddess, Caesar. Therefore, he cannot be my husband."

"Yes, so I have heard. But Sejanus didn't believe you. And, truthfully, I find it hard to believe myself."

"Nonetheless, Caesar, it is so. I am the goddess Antevorte, sometimes called Sylvia. It matters not whether humans believe this or not." Sylvia was grateful that it seemed Sejanus had not told Tiberius much about her. He didn't seem to know anything about the gun. Perhaps Sejanus was hoping to have some kind of advantage over Tiberius with this knowledge he kept to himself.

Tiberius rose from the couch and started to approach her with obvious intent. "I think I shall try to discover for myself if you are indeed what you claim to be."

Sylvia backed away. "Caesar, do not touch me. It would be hazardous to your health."

This clearly angered Tiberius. "You presume too much on my forbearance, Madam." He continued to approach.

"Caesar! Stop!" She pointed to one of his guards. "Have this man touch me, for your own sake, and see what happens. Make certain he attempts to touch one of my erogenous zones."

Tiberius hesitated. Her positive manner was making him cautious. He ordered the guard to touch her. Upon doing so, the guard immediately went into convulsions. She pushed him away so that he wouldn't be electrocuted to death.

Tiberius startled. "I don't understand. How can this be? How is it that Sejanus did not believe you?" He thought some more. "How is it you have a human lover, this Marcellus?"

Sylvia was prepared with a lie for this eventuality. "He does not touch me in this way. We are not lovers, though we do love each other. We allowed Sejanus to believe otherwise to protect Marcellus. We even feigned the appropriate noises for the guards outside our room. We are very, very careful in this. Prolonged improper contact would be the death of Marcellus." She fervently prayed he was gullible enough to believe this harebrained story.

Her demonstration of power inclined Tiberius to believe her. "I still don't understand. Then why did Sejanus keep you alive? Indeed, why should I keep you alive? Or if I am not able to kill you, why should I keep your man alive?"

"There are a couple of reasons. Firstly, it would have been dangerous for Sejanus to attempt to harm either one of us. I would not have been pleased and that is usually not good for the health of the person who has caused my displeasure. Secondly, I made a deal with Sejanus. I would tell him what was about to come, about the future."

Tiberius frowned. "If this is so, how is it I was able to have him executed, if he was forewarned?"

"Simple. I chose not tell him about this particular event. Sejanus was dangerous. I never trusted him fully to keep his part of the bargain. He was not stable. In my mind, he was better off dead. I decided you would be a better person to deal with."

She decided to take a gamble. "You are lecherous, and depraved." She gazed at him intently, "But you are not overly ambitious. You are not as impulsive as Sejanus. You are stable. If you agree not to harm Marcellus or attempt to harm me, I will warn you of events to come."

"How dare you!" shouted Tiberius.

Sylvia fought to hide her terror. She looked at him haughtily. "You are merely human. I have no reason to fear you. You are also smart enough to realize the great advantages you would gain from this deal."

This mollified him a bit. "If I agree to this, will you also find it advantageous to hide the circumstances of my own death?"

"I will tell you the details of your death right now, if you so wish."

Tiberius thought a bit. "No, I don't really want to know when I die. I just want to know if my death is the result of foul play."

"Very well then. You will die of natural causes. I won't tell you when." This was somewhat of a lie. Some historians have suggested that Caligula might have smothered him when he was ill. Sylvia saw no reason to tell him the truth.

"What of the glass?" asked Tiberius. "This is the original reason Sejanus had you arrested, is it not?"

"You mean the unbreakable glass?" she scoffed. "It does not exist, as far as I can see," she lied some more. Again, she saw no reason to reveal she suspected him of having killed Atticus.

Of course, this raised Tiberius's suspicions. *If she is what she claims to be, how is it she doesn't know what really happened? Also, what reason does she have to remain here in the human world, if she believes the glass does not exist? Still, it would be wise to go ahead with this bargain and see what happens.*

"I am agreed, goddess. We have a deal." *At least for the time being,* he thought.

Chapter 16

Isle of Capri 31 CE

"The gods be damned, woman! How did you ever convince the old bastard this wasn't happening?" He gasped, after a particularly intense bout of lovemaking.

"I am the happiest virgin who has ever lived," she laughed. "Still, we really have to be careful this time. That is why I have started to place this towel under us and why I'm so careful to keep it out of sight before I am able to clean it. And thank goodness we are able to lock this door."

Tiberius did remain fooled. He thought he knew better than the guards when they kept reporting that the two were indeed making love, and often at that. He had ordered their bed sheets repeatedly inspected and this had convinced him Sylvia had spoken the truth. Besides, hadn't she told him that they fake the noises of lovemaking?

"Still, my love, we have to be very careful. Tiberius is not fully convinced that I am a goddess. Hopefully, as I prove myself to be useful to him, it won't matter as much. But for now, it does."

"I agree completely, my dearest Amazon."

She laughed at this and then started to ponder this man who had become the best lover she had ever experienced. And the dearest. "Tell me more about yourself, Marcellus. You rarely speak about your past. You were married, were you not?"

"Perhaps that is because it is somewhat painful. Yes, I was married. Her name was Antonina. I also had a son, Pilius. They both died five years ago of some strange disease that took them quickly. They both developed blisters all over their bodies, and before I knew it, it was over. I really don't know how I survived after that.   I was a mess for the whole first year after."

Smallpox, she thought. "Oh Marcellus, I am so sorry. I should never have brought it up," she said.

"It is still painful to think of it. The gods must have sent you to help me. For the first time in years, I am happy, truly happy," he replied, smiling at her, "even if we are always in so much danger."

She moved over to him and hugged him tightly. "Maybe I shouldn't admit this, but I am in love with you, Marcellus. This is something new for me. I have never felt like this before."

Marcellus was surprised at her pronouncement. He didn't reply immediately. He remained pensive. "The men of your time must be fools. I don't really understand how all of this has happened. You were incredibly annoying to me at first, making all these demands and arrogantly forcing me to comply. Then, slowly, I started to learn to respect you. I really started to like you when I saw how kindly you were treating Marcipor."

Finally, he said, looking deeply into her eyes, "I think I started to love you when I realized you were human, not a goddess. I couldn't help but notice how kind and loving your soul was. Yes, Sylvia, it should be already obvious, but I am in love with you also."

His pronouncement caused her to tear up. *But I'm supposed to leave here and complete my mission. How will I ever be able to do that? If I am truthful to myself, I should be returning now. The mission is already completed. I can make my report to Tegar. The glass did exist but the formula is now beyond our reach. I suppose if he wishes to create a paradox, he could send me or someone else a little further back than when I first arrived. We now know the name of the man who invented it and location of his shop, but that decision is beyond my pay grade. Meanwhile, I really should be returning.*

She looked over at Marcellus. *And if I leave now, what would happen to him? He would be killed for sure.* She looked at him fiercely. *I could never do that. Never! He is my life. He is my reason for living right now.*

Marcellus did not miss the ferocity of her look. "What is it, my love? What vexes you?"

She laughed ruefully. "It is nothing, Marcellus, except maybe wondering what is taking you so long to start act two," she said, grinning impishly at him. He needed no further encouragement, but never noticed the tears in her eyes as they made love.

The weeks passed. Caligula started to notice that this very beautiful woman, supposedly a goddess, was avoiding him whenever possible. It was a morning on the second month, when she noticed Caligula approaching her from the other end of the hall. It was too late to turn around without being overly conspicuous.

She tried to get around him, but he kept moving to block her. Caligula laughed, "Hold, my lady. Whatever have I done to offend you? Do not my looks please you?" In truth, Caligula was a pretty handsome young man.

"Oh no, my lord. I have been very busy, is all."

"Yes, I can well imagine. Marcellus is a lucky man. You are a very beautiful woman." He looked at her lecherously. "I can think of ways to make you even busier."

Dammit, she thought. *I'm not wearing my special tunic. Stupid me! I should always be wearing it whenever there is a Caligula in the house.*

He grabbed her around the waist and pulled her to him. She struggled to get free while he proceeded to rub her bottom lasciviously. "My Lord," she shouted, "Let me go! I belong to another man!"

"That is of no matter to me. You shall now learn what a real lover is like." She continued to squirm and struggle. He just laughed and forced her to the floor. He pulled up her tunic and momentarily hesitated at the strange garment she was wearing underneath, having never seen modern panties. He pulled them down.

Oh my God! He's going to rape me, she sickeningly thought. She twisted this way and that to avoid penetration by his engorged penis. Suddenly, Caligula went flying off her. Marcellus had dealt him a solid blow to the side of his head. She turned to see her lover standing over Caligula.

"I would advise you not to try getting up, my Lord, if you wish to remain in one piece," he hissed angrily.

Caligula looked up at him in disbelief. "Your life is over. You do know that, don't you?" He then looked around, and shouted, "Guards! Guards, I have been attacked."

Three guards rushed up and two of them grabbed Marcellus by the arms, restraining him. The third looked at Sylvia and quickly surmised what must've happened. He was disgusted at Caligula, but knew he had to arrest her as well.

Tiberius was in a quandary. *Damn that fool boy. Goddess or no goddess, she has proven useful to me. She warned me of the invasion by Parthia and who knows what would've happened had I not been more prepared. Now what do I do?*

He sighed, "Bring them all in." The three participants in the previous day's folly entered. Caligula looked proud and angry. Marcellus looked a bit disdainful. Sylvia was terrified even though she was wearing her special tunic and had activated it earlier.

Before anyone else could say a word, Caligula sneered, "Caesar, this cretin, this peasant, struck me."

Tiberius looked at Marcellus. "Is this so?"

Marcellus looked haughtily at Caligula. "Yes, Caesar. He was trying to rape the goddess Antevorte. On the floor of one of your halls, I might add." He was starting to get angry again just thinking about it.

The Emperor's next statement surprised Caligula. "Gaius, have you not enough young ladies around willing to serve your every need? I would've thought it is most uncomely for a man of your position to force himself on an unwilling woman."

Caligula colored deeply. "She came on to me, Caesar."

"I most certainly did not!" shouted Sylvia, very indignant at the mere suggestion.

Tiberius looked sadly at Caligula. "Does it not seem unlikely to you, Gaius, that a lady would want to have sex on the hallway floor when there are plenty of more appropriate places available?"

Caligula started to protest but Tiberius stopped him. "Gaius, enough! It is clear what happened. Do not embarrass yourself further with some other poorly made up story."

"Antevorte, it appears you are not a goddess. Gaius managed to touch you."

"He did, Caesar, but fortunate for him, he had not yet touched the right places."

"That is a lie!" thundered Caligula.

"If it is a lie, then try to touch me now in an inappropriate place. Caesar, I need leave to hurt this man if he does so."

"You have it," he replied, thinking that maybe this young snot needed a lesson.

Caligula approached confidently. Hadn't he rubbed her bottom yesterday with no ill effect? He reached out and had barely touched her breast when the electricity flowed agonizingly through him. She was very tempted to just let him be electrocuted to death but knew she couldn't. The horrible implications to the timeline would be massive. Bad as he was, Caligula was destined to be the third emperor. She could not change that.

Tiberius was a bit concerned to see Caligula lying unconscious on the floor. Sylvia, realizing his concern, reassured, "He will be all right, Caesar, though I could have killed him if I so desired."

He then addressed Marcellus. "It seems that your interference was not required. You have struck a lord and that cannot go unpunished. Ten lashes, to be administered immediately. Guards, seize him, and bare his back."

Sylvia started to protest. She started to move forward but one of the guards blocked her path, careful not to touch her. She also wished to avoid touching him so they did kind of a weird dance back and forth. Meanwhile, Tiberius removed his sash and advanced to the bound Marcellus. He struck Marcellus lightly on the back, and counted, "One."

Realizing what was happening, Sylvia relaxed, while Tiberius tapped Marcellus lightly on his back nine more times while counting aloud.

"This won't be so symbolic, if it should happen again," he warned the two of them. He pointed to the prone Caligula. "I promise you he will not bother you again. You may go."

Sylvia couldn't help worrying. *He's going to be the next Emperor and I don't think he's the type to forgive and forget. Well, we still have a few years. As much as I hate it, I'll have to try and befriend the little bastard before that happens.*

Chapter 17

Isle of Capri 33 CE

A couple of years passed without any untoward incidents. Life continued as normally as possible, considering the strange circumstances the two lived under.

Sylvia was mostly pretty happy but sometimes she missed things from her previous life in the 21st century. She used to love going to the movies. Roman theater was a poor substitute. She loved flying. That wasn't going to happen soon. And then there were the small things that turned out to be not so small. Toilet paper. Good Lord, how she missed it. The stick with a sponge was a poor substitute. Decent underwear. The Roman equivalents were okay but not as good as the modern equivalents. Brassieres were nonexistent, as an example. Marcellus could not understand why she always insisted on binding her breasts. *No sagging for me,* was her raison d'etre. They weren't allowed to travel too much and when they did, it was always under guard. She fretted at how long it took to get anywhere. She never thought she would miss automobiles and traffic. Most worrisome was the lack of modern medicine. There were a lot of things that could kill you here which were minor annoyances in her time. She did have some antibiotic with her and was fortunate enough not to have to use any of it yet. She knew the antibiotics probably had an expiry date but she was confident they would work anyway if needed. She was careful as hell in her daily life. A broken leg or arm would be a disaster here.

What bothered her the most was the attitude many displayed toward Marcellus. She refused to play the part of the subservient Roman wife and he suffered for it. He had to endure comments about his lack of manliness, how he didn't know how to handle a difficult wife. Sylvia was aware of this, but there was nothing she could really do if she was to continue in the role of a powerful goddess, even though she knew many didn't even believe this. At least she wasn't in ancient Greece. This would've proven to be magnitudes of time more difficult.

There were things to like, however. She really appreciated how quiet it was. No traffic noises, no horns, no passing roar of airplanes, no beeps and boops from cell phones. Even the few times she was in Rome itself, the bustle of people was all she heard. And the air was wonderful. It was so clean. It smelled terrific. The only exception was when she was in the busiest parts of the city of Rome itself, but otherwise, there was no pollution whatsoever.

Sylvia's attempt to befriend Caligula had been an abysmal failure. He had obeyed Tiberius's command to leave them alone, but barely. He continually showed open hostility toward the two. He almost always managed to bump Sylvia when passing her in a hallway. This would almost always be followed with a sarcastic, "Oh, excuse me, your highness." She worried about this. What would happen when he became emperor? They surely would have to make themselves scarce.

He's such a petty baby, she mused after one such encounter. *It's hard to fathom that this child will soon become Emperor of one of the greatest empires in the history of mankind. It's funny. Some historians think he only became a monster after the fever that almost killed him six months into his reign. If only they knew. His good behavior at first was probably just a sham so that his ascent to the throne would not be opposed. But Marcellus and I know the real Caligula. He willfully takes part in all the sick depredations Tiberius manages to concoct almost daily. He's a psychopath, no doubt.*

She sighed. *It's really difficult living here in the palace, despite all the luxury and opulence. Thank God for Marcellus. I love him so much, it almost hurts. There is no way I can ever leave him now. It won't matter if I manage to extricate him from our dangerous situation. He is my husband, in fact, if not in name. Tegar will probably think I was killed, and that's okay with me. Who cares about a fucking glass! I have Marcellus in my life and that's all that counts.*

She was so lost in her thoughts that she almost didn't notice the elderly man who was approaching until he was nearly upon her. "If I c-could have a w-word with you, g-goddess?" He stammered.

He's stammering and he was limping. Oh my God, this must be Claudius! He is going to be Emperor after Caligula and he's going to be a good one for a change. It's really sad that his fourth wife will end up poisoning him so that her son, Nero, can become Emperor.

She smiled at him. "Of course, Claudius. I will always have time for you."

He started, wondering how she knew who he was. He was so recluse that the general public did not know about his stammering, so it couldn't be that. Of course, it was always possible she had heard about him in the two years she had lived here. "I have c-come here with the s-specific intention of interviewing you. P-please excuse my im-impertinence but I have heard you c-claim to be a g-goddess. I am not s-sure if I b-believe that."

She smiled at him again. "I don't blame you for being skeptical. People think you are addled, but I know better. I think skepticism is the sign of a rational and intelligent mind."

Claudius found himself liking this woman and not because she was beautiful or that she was praising him. He had originally thought she was a charlatan, feeding on the superstition dominant in this age. Yet he couldn't deny she seemed to know things that she shouldn't.

"D-do you really c-claim to be a g-goddess?"

She stared at him intently, making him a bit uncomfortable. "I do claim that," she answered simply. "But think on this, Claudius. Imagine a future, a future 2,000 years from now, where traveling through time is possible, where it would be possible to go back to a previous era in history. If a person from that time came to a more primitive culture, what role would be most efficacious for that person?" She was wondering if he was intelligent enough to figure out where she was going with this.

It was Claudius's turn to stare. He had already interviewed Tiberius who had been pretty annoyed and impatient through it all. Tiberius had reluctantly claimed she had foretold events that came to pass. Claudius was indeed a very intelligent person and quick to grasp things. *Of course! Now it all makes sense. If what Tiberius claims is true, then a person from the future would know what was going to happen and I think that is what she is implying in a very subtle way. This is a matter of future science and not mythical entities. Will man be able to do this in the future? Travel in time? And to this matter, what is she doing here?*

"I c-can imagine that, m-my lady. What I d-don't understand is why s-such a p-person would c-come here."

"It is of no importance why such a person would come here. A piddling matter anyway. But you can be confident that such a person would intend no harm, and would be very careful not to do anything that would change the historical course of events."

This got Claudius thinking. *This all made sense even if it was almost impossible to believe. If a person did indeed come from the future, they would not do anything to change the course of history. Otherwise their own world would be changed. In fact, their very existence might be threatened.* Claudius knew he was not going to get anything more out of her. It unsettled him a bit that she wouldn't reveal her purpose in being here. He had never been a good judge of character but he did believe and trust her. It had taken just this brief encounter for him to come to this conclusion.

"So b-be it. I w-wish you a g-good day, m-my lady." He started to limp away while Sylvia stood there, rather pensive.

"Claudius, if I may have a further word."

He stopped, and returned to her. "Y-yes?"

She remained silent for a moment. The strange look she gave him unsettled him a bit. "W-what is it, m-my lady?"

"If I may make a suggestion for your research." Sylvia was aware that Claudius did a lot of research for his books. "I think you should study more about affairs of state, governance, diplomacy, etc. Things like that, you know."

At first puzzled, understanding slowly grew on Claudius. His eyes widened. "N-no! Th-this is a thing I d-do not want!" He liked his present life. There was no doubt in what she was foretelling.

"What we want and what we get, are often not the same, Claudius. In any event, if your research is to be deeply effective, you should take eight years."

Claudius understood immediately. He would become Emperor in eight years, if he understood this properly. He looked so glum that Sylvia felt compelled to add, "Not all emperors are bad. Some turn out to be surprisingly good." Claudius just nodded, grateful for that last tidbit.

I don't have the heart to tell him he will be poisoned by his fourth wife and besides, such knowledge would undoubtedly affect the timeline. He is a good man and doesn't deserve this, she unhappily thought, as she watched him slowly walk away.

Chapter 18

Isle of Capri 35 CE

Sylvia was pregnant and it was beginning to show. Caligula was delighted. He knew Tiberius would be furious as the old fool had insisted on believing there was nothing physical going on between her and Marcellus. He proved to be completely right as Sylvia was summoned to Tiberius.

Upon entering the room, she could see that Tiberius was very angry. Before she could say a word, he roared, "You lied to me, you fucking bitch! You made me look like a goddamn fool. Everybody tried to tell me you were fucking Marcellus. But stupid me, I took you at your word. I believed you."

"Tiberius, I-"

"Shut your fucking mouth! I should have you put to death. No, even worse than that, I should execute Marcellus and have you watch."

"Tiberius, listen, I-"

"And why should I listen to you, when every word that comes out of your mouth is a fucking lie," he seethed. He gave her a very dangerous look. "We both know you are too valuable to me to kill you. However, now that I know you are able to partake in carnal events…" He started to advance on her.

Sylvia was terrified. Her special tunic had lost its functionality and been discarded years ago. She backed up slowly, thinking furiously. In as brave a voice as she could muster, she whispered, "Tiberius, I will not submit to this."

He laughed. "And just what do you think you can do to stop me?"

"If you do this, I shall no longer be your advisor. I am aware this will result in my death, but I promise you, I care not."

He stopped, and looked at her carefully. He could see she was serious. "So, you would rather die than fuck me," he angrily snapped.

"This has nothing to do with you personally. I would rather die than have relations with any other man except Marcellus. He is more than my lover. He is my life."

He stood there undecided. He was a bit mollified. She continued, "So far, I have helped you prevent an invasion and I have foiled an assassination attempt. Is it worth it for you to lose this just for a roll in the hay?" Of course, Tiberius had no way of knowing he would've accomplished this without her help, according to historical records.

He didn't even bother to threaten Marcellus. He knew her response would be the same. Nevertheless, he couldn't just let this go. "You are correct, bitch. I will let you both live and I won't touch you. However, you have lost my favor. You will be removed from your present room and reassigned to a room in the servants' quarters. You will no longer dine with us. You will take your meals with the servants. And when the time comes for your baby to enter the world, you will receive no help from us. You and Marcellus will be on your own. Is this understood?"

"Yes, Caesar." She didn't mind this at all. She felt a sense of profound relief that she or Marcellus weren't going to be executed. It could've been much worse.

"Now go," he thundered. "And try to keep out of my sight unless summoned by me or you have something important to report."

She bowed and left the room.

The baby girl was born a few months later. Fortunately, the birth had not been a difficult one. There had been no complications and Marcellus had proven to be a decent midwife. They named her, Livia. It was Marcellus who had insisted on this name. Upon seeing the flaming red hair on his newborn daughter, he had to be dissuaded from calling her Sylvia. The name Livia was a compromise.

They both doted on their daughter. Their poor accommodations and scant meals didn't bother them in the least. The little girl was the joy in their lives. Nothing else mattered to them.

Marcellus knew Sylvia would be a wonderful mother and he was not disappointed. Some of her actions surprised him. She changed the baby frequently. After cleaning the cloth diapers, she would boil them in water. When he asked her why she was doing this, she started explaining about tiny creatures called bacteria. It took him a bit of time to understand what she was talking about and even then, he found it a little hard to believe. There were creatures too tiny to see who lived in our bodies and could cause disease. Yet some of these creatures were good and necessary for our well-being. He found it uncomfortable to think about, creatures crawling all over his body.

"Are you certain about this, sweetheart?"

"For God sakes, Marcellus, how often are you going to doubt me about this? When have I been wrong about anything concerning science?"

"It just seems so impossible."

"Marcellus, how many children today die before they reach the age of five? I mean, out of 10, how many would you say don't make it?"

"Why are you asking this?"

"Humor me, will you. Just answer the question."

"I'm no doctor, you understand, but based on what I've seen, I'd say three or four."

"Exactly. In my time, do you know how many die out of 10?"

He smiled. "No, but I bet I'm about to find out."

"Less than one. And that's because we make sure the harmful bacteria is killed before it can infect our babies. Boiling water kills bacteria, as does soap."

"Aha! So that's why you insist on me washing my hands all the time."

"Yes."

"But I don't understand how these bacteria can get past the skin of my hands."

"It can't. It just stays alive until you move your hand to your mouth, which everyone does frequently, by the way. It then moves onto your mouth and into your system."

By 18 months, Livia was walking fairly confidently. She loved to play the game where Marcellus was pretending to chase her but just couldn't catch her. He would graze his hand down her running back as if he almost had her. She would shriek and arch her back as she picked up her speed. Sylvia couldn't help smiling as she watched them play in this way.

Sylvia's favorite game was to pick up her child, bring her close, and blow into her stomach. This would cause Livia to thrust her head back and burst into giggles. There was little doubt that their world revolved around Livia.

Marcellus was busy building a new cabinet which he felt would make things easier. Sylvia had just come home from helping the servants with some of their chores. It drove her crazy to just do nothing, so when not involved with Livia, she had taken to helping the servants.

"So where is the little munchkin?" She asked, after kissing Marcellus.

"She's playing down in her little corner with her doll." Livia had taken the small space between the bed and the wall as her kingdom.

Sylvia moved there. "Marcellus, she's not there."

"Damn, I warned her too many times not to wander out without us. I might have to spank her this time," said Marcellus sighing.

"Not while there's breath in my body," hissed Sylvia. "My child does not get spanked."

Marcellus didn't want to reopen this argument before finding Livia. He considered methods of child-rearing in her time to be soft and liable to create a spoiled child.

"LIVIA… LIVIA," he yelled out loud, trying to locate her.

"She's probably hiding. You know how she likes that game." But Sylvia was starting to get worried. "Come on out, honey. I have some nice grapes for you." This always worked, but not this time.

Their room wasn't very large so it didn't take long for their complete inspection. They started to become truly frightened as they realized Livia was missing. They began searching the entire palace. Sylvia had plenty of help. She was very popular with the servants so many of them were looking with her.

Hours passed, but still no Livia. Finally, two of the servants approached Marcellus and Sylvia. They became very alarmed, as one of the women was crying. The one named Octavia pointed to the crying woman. "This is Camilla. She has some news," she said sadly.

The sobbing woman took some moments to settle herself down. Finally, she was able to speak. "I saw your daughter (sniff) walking with Caligula. He was holding her hand (sniff)."

A cold dagger went through Marcellus's heart. Sylvia's eyes widened and she began to tremble. Camilla continued her story. "They walked to the balcony. He was pretending (sniff) to be friendly with her. Then he, oh the gods! How can I say this?" Her voice broke and she started to cry again. "He picked her up and," she looked at both of them, and could barely get it out. In a very hushed and squeaky voice, she whispered, "He, he threw her over the cliffs."

Sylvia sank to the floor and just screamed. Marcellus went chalk white. "I'll kill him. This monster is dead," he hissed. He stalked out of the room, not even noticing his broken lover.

Sylvia's hysterical crying lasted for a few minutes before she became aware of Marcellus's absence. "Where did he go?" she sobbed.

"He went that way," Octavia pointed down one of the halls. "But there's nothing down that way except for the kitchen."

Understanding came to Sylvia instantly. They had not been allowed any weapons, but all kitchens contained knives. She rose and hurried after him. She encountered him leaving the kitchen. He was carrying the largest knife he could find.

She blocked his path. "Marcellus, you can't!"

"We'll just see if I can't," he hissed. "I don't care if they kill us."

"That's not it, Marcellus. The timeline. He has to be the next Emperor."

"Fuck the timeline!" He bellowed. "Is that fucking timeline more important than our child?" He was looking at her accusingly.

"Nothing is more important than our child, Marcellus. You of all people know that. But if you kill Caligula now, you will kill millions and millions of people who were meant to be born, but won't be."

"I don't care," he shouted.

"You might even kill me," she said, looking deeply into his eyes. "There's even the possibility you wouldn't realize I had ever existed. Without Caligula, the timeline would be so radically changed that I doubt I would even be born. Do you realize the millions of perfect connections going all the way back to the beginning of time that have to be made, for a specific human to be born? Forget about just your parents meeting and making love at just the right time. Your grandparents also do. And your great-grandparents. The timing of lovemaking has to be precise all through the ages for a specific human to ultimately be born. In fact, I would say it's a certainty I wouldn't be born if you kill Caligula."

This stopped him cold. Frustrated tears came to his eyes. "So, I have to let this bastard live? Even though he's torn my heart from my body?"

They both burst into tears, slowly lowering themselves to the floor, hugging each other.

They spent days in profound mourning. Most days, Sylvia had to force herself to get out of bed. Sometimes, she would unexpectedly burst into tears. Usually, she just felt numb. Marcellus often disappeared for hours on end. He was a very proud man and Sylvia figured he just needed some private space to mourn.

It took over a week before Tiberius would even see her.

"That monster killed my baby," was the first thing she said to him.

 "Yes, I've heard," Tiberius coldly answered.

"Are you going to do anything about it?"

"No. He is royalty. The baby is not. The baby is of no consequence. Perhaps now, you can see the folly of having deceived me."

She looked at him in disbelief. She had approached him because she knew there would be no death sentence for Caligula, so the timeline would be safe. But she never expected this callous indifference. She turned and walked slowly away, thinking, *That such a petty and psychopathic man could be the Emperor of Rome!*

It was a testament to their great love for each other that the death of Livia did not split them apart. If anything, it drove them closer together.

Within a few months they were back to a semblance of normality. "I shall never forget Livia. She will always live in my heart, sweetheart, but we can take solace in the knowledge that there will be other babies," Marcellus said one day.

"Not here! Never here! Not while we're close to that bastard. And that brings me to something that we need to talk about. We have two years to figure out how to escape this godforsaken place. Tiberius will die in two years. Caligula will become the new Emperor. I don't have to tell you what will happen if we're still around when that happens. He hates us. He won't accept any deal with us."

“I know, my love. I know,” Marcellus said, nodding. “One thing I do need for you to tell me. The exact date this bastard dies.” There was steel in his eyes when he said this.

Chapter 19

Isle of Capri 36 - 37 CE

"It's November already, and we're no closer to getting away from this damn island than we were two years ago," Sylvia complained.

"It's not like I haven't tried, sweetheart. They're watching me everywhere I go."

"Yeah, but time is running out, Marcellus. Tiberius is going to die in March. That's just two months from now." (The Roman calendar only had 10 months, and March followed December). "We need to be away from here before Caligula assumes power. God knows, we'll be on the run regardless of whether we're here or not."

"I know, Sylvia. I know," he answered despondently.

"I could take you back to my time, Marcellus." She looked up at him, trying to gauge his reaction.

"And what would I do there? What would I be qualified to do? Two thousand years from now! I'd be like a baby. A helpless, astonished baby. And you've already told me this man Tegar would be very displeased. He would probably try to send me back. And based on what you've told me, you would lose your job and your income. No, I am not willing to do that."

Sylvia knew her man very well. She knew how proud he was. She knew it would be a waste of time arguing about it. She sighed, "You're right. Tegar would probably send you back, anyway." But deep inside, she felt that option was still open. If he was about to be killed or tortured, he was going back to her time, his pride be damned.

She grew pensive. "Look, lover, I might have a solution. But it's risky. Very risky."

He looked at her questioningly.

"There's a woman in the kitchen, a servant. Her name is Portia. I think she likes me. We get along famously. Now I realize she could be just a spy, reporting back to Tiberius or Caligula. But I think at this point, we just have to take the chance. We might be able to use her to bribe one of the fishermen."

"By the gods, Sylvia, that is taking a big risk! How well do you know this woman!"

"Tell me what choice we have!" She shouted, and then in a quieter voice, she hissed, "If you have a better idea, now's the time to tell me."

Marcellus just hung his head. "You know I don't."

"Okay then. I will need money."

He looked at her and nodded. He pulled back their bed and pried open a wooden plank on the floor. He never thought he would consider it lucky to be moved into this servants' room. There were no wooden planks in their former opulent quarters where they had no need to hide their money. Tiberius seemed to have forgotten that they had some money of their own. Or maybe he had never known. He was quite certain it would've been confiscated had Tiberius remembered once he discovered how they had been fooling him. Not that he needed the money. It would just be another punishment.

He retrieved two Aurii. "One should be enough for the fishermen. The other will be for that servant. You do realize what will happen if she reports us? He won't kill us. He still needs you. But I would be surprised if we're not chained to the wall when he's not using you."

She looked at him morosely. "I know, but what choice do we have?"

The next day Sylvia approached Portia. "I need to speak to you," she whispered. She looked around. "In private." Portia looked at her in surprise, and then nodded. The two women retreated to one of the kitchen pantries.

"We need to get off of this island, Portia," Sylvia whispered urgently.

"So-, so what does this have to do with me?" Portia already had pretty much figured it out, but she was afraid. She really didn't want to get involved.

"You know I'm watched wherever I go. I need you to take this money," she pulled the coins out from a pouch under her tunic. "And find a fisherman who will be willing to take us away."

"That is dangerous, my lady. I will be surely whipped if I am caught," she pleaded. "I was only whipped once before and I can assure you, I don't wish to repeat the experience."

"You think I don't know that, Portia! I hate having to ask you. But it's only a matter of time before Tiberius dies. And when that happens, Gaius will kill us. You have to know that."

Portia looked at her dubiously. Sylvia nodded. "Do not doubt this. He hates us. You know what he did to our baby. If Tiberius dies, and we're still here, I assure you, we will be killed. That is something beyond a doubt."

Portia sighed. She really liked Sylvia who was obviously highborn and yet had never talked down to her. Not only that, she had never considered herself above helping out in the kitchen. She gulped and then with a look of resolve, she said, "I'll do it."

"Oh, thank you, Portia! I-"

"Do not say another word, my lady, or I might change my mind. What you have asked scares me to death, but I have said I will do it, and that is enough."

Sylvia just nodded and then handed her the coins. "One should be enough for the fisherman. The other is for you."

Portia looked at the coins and then looked up at Sylvia. The Aurius would go a long way to buying her freedom. She just hugged Sylvia. "I will do my best, Mistress. May Jupiter protect the two of us."

"What you ask is dangerous, my little lady," warned the captain. "Why would I take that risk?"

"I can pay." Portia produced the auria.

The captain snatched it from her hand. "And how will you pay now?"

Portia was close to tears. It had been foolish of her to show the money before anything was settled. The captain may have been a bastard, but he did have a little sympathy in his black heart. "I'll tell you what," he said, looking her over and liking what he saw. "I'll take the two across, but there's a little more payment required. If you would follow me to my quarters."

Portia just sighed. This wasn't the first time she had been forced into this uncompromising situation. She meekly followed him up the gangplank. *I hope you're worth it, Mistress, for the price I'm now going to have to pay.*

Three days later, Sylvia rushed into the room and up to Marcellus. He could tell from the fire in her eyes that she was pretty excited. "We have a boat," was all she said. Portia never told her about the extra fee she had been forced to pay.

A month passed without anything significant happening. Sylvia had warned Marcellus that Tiberius would fall ill early in March and then be moved to his villa at Micenum on the mainland where he would die on the 17th.

"I think it would be best for us if we left a few hours after Tiberius is moved. Most of his retinue will be going with him. If there ever was a time when surveillance will be compromised, this is probably it," opined Sylvia. "We need to be ready then. I just wish I knew the exact date when he's being moved."

"But I assume you warned that fisherman we would be required to leave with just a few hours' notice."

"You know I did, Marcellus. Stop worrying about what I did or didn't do. I don't think I've become stupid in the last few months," she huffed, with a great deal of chagrin.

Marcellus was surprised at how she had snapped at him. *This stress is wearing on us all,* he surmised.

The day finally arrived. A large commotion filled the palace. It seemed a small army was preparing to leave. Marcellus and Sylvia looked at each other, scared but determined.

That night, they watched the whole entourage depart. Marcellus had just returned from a brief scouting mission. "Most of the guards are gone. The palace seems empty. We have to go now."

For the first time in years, there was no guard shadowing them as they crept down the hallway and up the stairs. Sylvia thought her heart would explode out of her chest, it was beating so hard. They were on the verge of exiting the palace and going down the trail to the sea. Marcellus stopped abruptly. "STOP! Stop," he urgently whispered. "There's just one guard. We'll have to wait for him to move."

A half-hour had passed. The guard hadn't moved. "For God's sake, when is the bastard going to leave?" Sylvia was growing increasingly impatient.

Marcellus turned to her. "I'm going to have to deal with him," he despondently said.

"Marcellus, you can't kill him! The damage to the timeline would be immense."

"I'll try, Sylvia. I'll try. But if it's between your timeline and our lives, you have to know what my choice is going to be."

Sylvia just sighed. *It's always "my" timeline, as if I'm responsible for it. I know he understands the significance of all of this, so I don't know why he gets passive aggressive when there's any mention of the timeline.*

Marcellus crept stealthily up to the back of the guard. He then dealt him a mighty blow to the back of his head. The guard fell down, somewhat dazed. Marcellus jumped on him, straddling him. He then started delivering powerful blows to the man's face. The guard didn't have a chance. He struggled vainly to get Marcellus off him. His wooziness soon turned to unconsciousness. Marcellus confiscated his gladius with scabbard and his pugio.

"Do not be concerned. He's alive. I don't know how long he'll be out, so we better get a move on."

Sylvia knew Marcellus had been a soldier. She knew he was brave. She knew he was strong. But she was still surprised at the level of violence he had just displayed. She knew it was necessary, but she still didn't like it.

Portia had detailed exactly where their ship was moored. The two of them simultaneously breathed a sigh of relief to see that the ship was indeed there when they arrived. The gangplank was already deployed. A solitary man was stationed at the end. "My name is Felix. I am the captain of this ship. And who might you be?"

"I am Marcellus, and this is Antevorte, or Sylvia, if you prefer."

The captain nodded. These were indeed the two who had paid for passage. "Do you have the rest of the money?" He asked.

"Rest of the money?" Marcellus asked, not understanding what was going on.

"The maid said it was one Aurius right away, and one at departure."

Sylvia and Marcellus looked at each other. "I don't think Portia would screw us like this," she whispered. "I think this captain is just getting greedy. I also don't think it's worth arguing about, out here in the open. I realize it hurts your pride, Marcellus, but it's better if we just pay him."

Marcellus scowled. He pulled an Aurius out of his pouch. There were a million things he wanted to say, but he didn't, as he handed over the money.

The voyage to the mainland was pleasant. The sea was very calm as there was no wind at all. It took a little under two hours. Sylvia and Marcellus were not having a pleasant time however. They were engaged in a bit of an argument.

"So, you're trying to tell me that slavery is wrong. Ridiculous." Marcellus was starting to get a little bit angry over this conversation. "How in Jupiter's name do you get any work done?"

"Yes, it's wrong. How can you think it's okay to take away a man's freedom, to make him work for free?"

"That man is either a criminal or someone captured in a war. If he's a slave, he deserves to be one." Marcellus couldn't believe she was arguing about this. It should have been self-evident.

"Oh, that's just great!" She gave him a thoroughly disgusted look.

He turned a bit red. "So, I'm to suppose you don't have slaves?"

"Of course, we don't have slaves. My country hasn't allowed slavery for 150 years. And something else, Marcellus, many of our states, what you call provinces, do not allow the execution of criminals. In fact, most countries around the world don't allow it."

"Why that's ridiculous! You allow murderers to live? People seem to have grown soft in your time. You have replaced justice with pity."

Sylvia grew silent. At first, she couldn't stand him. It took her a good hour to get over her anger. Reason eventually asserted itself. *He is the man I love. I can't blame him for the society in which he was raised. And I know him. Despite his draconian beliefs, he is kindhearted and loving. I need to avoid these conversations that solve nothing except highlighting that we are both from very different cultures.*

He was looking out at sea, his back turned to her. She reached up and pulled his shoulder back. He turned to her, displaying the same emotion of regret that she now felt. "I love you, you know," she whispered quietly.

"I love you, too," he answered simply, giving her a very tender look. "we should not argue over stupid things."

They had not noticed the captain who had witnessed the entire scene. *Yep, those two are married for sure. First an argument, then this. I'd like to be a fly in their bedroom tonight.* He smiled at the thought.

As agreed, they were dropped off just short of the port in Sorrento. There was no need for more people than necessary to see them disembarking.

They both realized they couldn't even trust this Captain or his men, especially if some sort of reward was eventually offered.

They figured they had some time before Caligula would turn his thoughts to them. Marcellus wanted to see his old shop, so the next day, they carefully made their way to it. They passed a crier on their way. "Hear ye, hear ye," he shouted. "It is with great pleasure I announce Gaius Caesar Germanicus has been named your next Emperor. Long live Caesar!"

The people nearby actually applauded. His father, Germanicus had been a folk hero to the Roman people. They thought his son would be the same.

So Tiberius is finally dead, thought Sylvia.

~~~~~~~~~~~~~~~~~~~~~~~~~~~~~~~~~~~~

Caligula was pacing the floor in the hallway just outside the room where Tiberius was dying. *Why doesn't the old bastard just hurry up and die,* he thought impatiently. The entire entourage had been moved to Misenum just a few days before. Caligula couldn't wait to become Emperor. True, he would be nominally only a co-emperor. Tiberius had also named his 18-year-old grandson, Gemellus as co-emperor. *That's a problem easily solved,* mused Caligula. *The old bastard must've been demented in these last few months. How could he not realize he was bestowing on his grandson a death sentence?*

One of the doctors exited the room. "The Emperor is dead," he announced.

Caligula had to suppress the urge to clap. He pretended to be mournful. "We must make preparations for the body," he said sadly.

He entered the room and walked up to the body. He asked all to leave so he could pay proper respects. He looked down on Tiberius. *You certainly took your time, you old bastard. Now it's my turn.*

Suddenly, Tiberius gasped and took a deep breath. He attempted to sit up.

By all the gods, how can this be? thought Caligula, clearly startled. He gazed thoughtfully at Tiberius and quickly made up his mind. *You've had your day, old man.* He pushed Tiberius back down onto the bed. He
~~~~~~~~~~~~~~~~~~~~~~~~~~~~~~~~~~~~

grabbed his pillow and slammed it over Tiberius's head, and began smothering him. Tiberius struggled weakly but soon remained still. *The universe is back in its proper place,* thought Caligula. Tiberius was 77.

~~~~~~

Marcellus asked, "I've been meaning to ask you," Why do you refer to Gaius as Caligula? That was a nickname given to him when he was a child," inquired Marcellus.

"If you ask anyone in my time who was Gaius Caesar Germanicus, no one would know. Now, if you said Caligula, most people would recognize him," she answered.

"That is indeed an irony," mused Marcellus.

"Believe me, he turns out to be quite the monster. If he is doomed to be deprecated by this nickname, I would call that justice."

They weren't too concerned about being apprehended at this point. Caligula would have too much on his plate to be concerned with them right now. That would change, of course. It is doubtful they would've chanced a visit to Marcellus's old shop later on.

They were surprised to find the shop open, and serving wine. And it was Marcipor who was doing the serving.

Marcipor looked up and started. "Marcellus!" He barely got out. "Is it really you?"

Marcellus smiled. "Yes, Marcipor, it is me. And this is Sylvia. She is not a goddess, you should know. She is my wife, though we are not legally married."

Marcipor moved forward and hugged them both. "It pleases me so to see you alive. Truth be told, I thought you were dead, having never heard from you these last six years."
~~~~~~

He hesitated, and then continued, "This shop is yours, of course. I have just been taking care of it. I came back when it became obvious there was no longer any danger here."

Marcellus just smiled. "That is magnanimous of you, Marcipor, but this place is now more yours than mine. If it is acceptable to you, I would like to propose a partnership. Obviously, Sylvia and I will still have to be absentee as long as Gaius is Emperor."

"You got in trouble with him too?"

Sylvia had to suppress the urge to laugh. *He thinks we're a trouble magnet, and I can't say I really blame him.*

"We have been on the Isle of Capri with him for the last six years. Do not believe what you think you know about Gaius. The man is a monster. He killed our baby, threw her over a cliff."

Marcipor gasped.

Marcellus continued, "And he took part in many of Tiberius's depredations. He hates us because he tried to rape Sylvia, that is her true name by the way, not Antevorte, and I punched him to prevent this atrocity. Later on, Sylvia shocked him unconscious. He has hated us from that time."

Sylvia chimed in, "He continually bumps me in the hallways and he insults us every chance he gets." She continued, "He will appear to be great for the first six months or so. Do not be fooled. The monster will eventually make an appearance. Many will die under his reign, even more than under either Sejanus or Tiberius."

"Yet, Marcellus says you are not a goddess, so how would you know this?" Marcipor asked reasonably.

"Never mind, Marcipor. It's a long story. We will stay here for a couple of nights. We think that's safe. And then we'll move on. Hopefully, someday, I'll be able to return and take up my part of the partnership. For now, Marcipor, all profits are yours." Marcellus appeared adamant in this.

Marcipor started to object. Marcellus held up his hand. "We have plenty of money. Do not worry about that. Right now, you're doing all the work, so you should have all the money. I'll begin taking my share once I return and start working with you."

"But-"

"This conversation is over," interrupted Marcellus. Marcipor just sighed.

They left the shop a few days later. "You know, last time we tried to run, we were correctly anticipated by the Emperor and were caught. I think we have to do something different this time," mused Sylvia.

Marcellus grew pensive. "I have an uncle in Ardea. That's just south of here. We could try there. I'm not sure if he would take us in, but he might. Let's try that first."

Chapter 20

Ardea 37 CE

It was with a great deal of trepidation, Marcellus approached the villa of his uncle, Marius. He hardly knew the man even though he was his father's brother. He suspected his father and uncle might've had some kind of falling out. His villa looked prosperous, solidly middle-class. The farm was doing well.

Marcellus pounded on the wooden door. After a minute or so, a man in his late middle ages appeared. "Yes?" said Marius. "And who are you?"

"Marcellus," he answered, looking somewhat sheepish.

"Marcellus who?" His uncle still hadn't recognized him.

"Marcellus Pontius Silanus," he blandly replied.

Marius took a double take. "You are my brother's son?" he whispered.

"Yes, uncle, I am."

Marius stared at him for a long, uncomfortable moment. Then he gingerly approached, took the younger man into his arms and hugged him.

"And who is this beautiful young woman?" His uncle asked, clearly admiring Sylvia.

"She is my wife, Sylvia." Marcellus found no reason to reveal they weren't legally married. He had noticed Marius's look. He was taking no chances. He had no idea what his uncle's sexual propensities might be but by branding her as his wife, he was establishing her as untouchable.

Sylvia understood perfectly what was going on. She played the naïve fool. "I thank you sir, for your compliment," she answered innocently.

Marius just smiled. "Come in, come in," he said, beckoning them inside. "Please, sit." Then he called out, "Valentina, come, please. We have guests."

A dark-haired, olive-skinned beauty who couldn't be older than 25, made her appearance. Marcellus was pretty sure his uncle was north of 50. Marius did not miss the look on his nephew's face. "Your dear aunt Octavia died three years ago of consumption. I was lucky enough to have Valentina come into my life." Valentina had previously been Octavia's chief maid.

Marcellus did not miss the once-over Valentina gave him. *And I'm sure she was lucky enough to have found you. A trophy wife and a gold digger. Such a cliché,* he thought unkindly.

"Valentina, this is my nephew, Marcellus, and his beautiful wife, Sylvia."

"You are welcome, both of you," she enthused. But Sylvia did not miss the brief, cold look Valentina gave her.

About a half-hour had passed in small talk. "Uncle, you might not be so welcoming when you hear what I have to say. We need your help. We need sanctuary."

"What-, what is it? What has happened?"

"The new Emperor, Gaius Caesar, wants us dead."

"For whatever reason? What have you done?" Going along with the public's initial high regard for Caligula, his uncle assumed Marcellus must have done something wrong.

"We have done nothing, except perhaps, not allowing him to rape Sylvia."

Marius just shook his head. "I find it hard to believe that a fine young man like Gaius would even attempt a thing like this."

"He is not a fine young man," interjected Sylvia. "We have been on the Isle of Capri with him for the last six years. He did try to rape me. I was fortunate that Marcellus heard the commotion and intervened."

"But that is not all, uncle. Tiberius's palace was worse than any brothel one can imagine. The filthy depredations were continual. Gaius was a willing participant in all of it. But there is one more thing which is even worse. He killed our baby girl. He threw her over a cliff." Marcellus was tearing up. He could barely get the last part out.

Marius gasped, and put his hand on Marcellus's shoulder.

Valentina showed no sympathy whatsoever. She piped up, "This would be very dangerous, Marius."

"Yes, it would. And I understand completely, uncle, if you show us the door." Marius could tell the young man was sincere.

Marius looked intently at the two fugitives. *This **would** be very dangerous. Yet, they have done nothing wrong. And they are family*. He smiled. "I would be haunted by the ghost of my brother forever if I did not take you in. You are always welcome here."

Valentina could not hide the look of disgust she briefly showed. *Oh well, at least there's that hunk of a man, Marcellus. It will be delicious to seduce him. I just know it. Be a welcome change from that old fart.*

A month had passed and the two had settled in well with their uncle. Marius had periodically sent one of his slaves into Rome to find out if there was any news about his new guests. So far, they were not on any proscription lists.

"Are you sure Gaius wants you dead?" Marius asked Marcellus one day while they were working in the field. "Maybe he's forgotten about you."

"As sure as I know the sun will rise tomorrow and he is not one to forget a slight," bleakly answered Marcellus.

"Uncle, I punched him, and later on, Sylvia shocked him into unconsciousness. He wants to kill us. Trust me."

Shocked him into unconsciousness. What the hell does that mean, thought Marius. "But so far, he's been a terrific Emperor. He's canceled all the treason trials. He's held some games. He's started some building."

"Yes, Sylvia told me he would be exemplary for his first six months."

Marius looked at him strangely. "We need to talk about Sylvia. This is not the first time you have hinted she knows things which she shouldn't."

Marcellus sighed. His uncle had harbored them, putting himself at great risk. He deserved to know the truth. "Uncle, you are going to find this hard to believe." He sighed again. "Sylvia, is not from our time. She is from 2,000 years in the future."

His uncle frowned. "I don't understand. What do you mean?"

"Sylvia is a time traveler. Two thousand years from now, they will have developed the science necessary to travel through time. She has read all about what is happening now in her history books."

Marius chuckled. "I'm afraid I am finding this hard to believe."

"We will be able to provide proof once we get back to the house. For the time being, believe me when I say, Gaius is being good now and will continue in this way for the next few months. He will then get a fever or be poisoned, future historians aren't sure, but he will survive it. And once he does, he becomes a monster. By the way, you might find this somewhat funny. Most people in the future have never heard of Gaius Caesar Germanicus. They all know him by his nickname, Caligula."

His nephew seemed so sure of himself. Gaius wondered if he spoke truth or if he was insane. Or maybe he had been beguiled by this woman, Sylvia.

He got his answer a few hours later. After hugging and kissing Sylvia, Marcellus asked her to retrieve her computer/mirror. She gave him a significant look, nodding slightly towards Marius. "He needs to know, sweetie. It is time."

She retrieved the mirror. "What would you like me to show him, Marcellus?"

"Oh, I don't know. Maybe a typical scene from one of your cities."

She beckoned Marius to come closer. He was already pretty intrigued, but completely skeptical. *That's just a mirror. What's it going to do? Fly away?*

"Computer, show a typical New York City street scene," she commanded in English. Marius noted the strange language and then he peered in. It took him a few seconds to understand what he was seeing. But slowly, he began to comprehend. Understanding slowly turned into amazement. *This mirror is showing theater!*

"Why, those are vehicles that move without horses. And those buildings are incredible. They soar into the sky."

"Sylvia, show him an airplane taking off and then landing."

She did so. Marius felt his knees go weak as he saw this huge vessel rise into the sky, and then later on, he saw this vessel come back down and gently kiss the earth. Marius was speechless. He just turned his head and looked closely at Sylvia.

Before he could say a word, Marcellus bade Sylvia give him a weather report for the week. The computer did so, indicating there would be thunderstorms tomorrow. Marius started. This was the first time the computer had actually spoke. Finally, Sylvia commanded, "Computer, when were you built?"

"I was built by Tegar industries on April 15, 2020. I achieved consciousness on July 7, 2020."

The dates were meaningless to Marius. "They count dates starting from just 37 years before this time. So, they start counting from our 716, that is, our 716 is their first year. Sylvia comes from 2021 in their way of counting, 2737 in ours. (The Romans started counting from the year they believed Rome was founded, 753 BCE). They have a religious reason for this which I'll explain later," offered Marcellus. "But if they call 37 years ago, year one, then I'm sure you can work out Sylvia is from 2,000 years in the future."

Having seen the mirror work, it was impossible for Marius to discount what his nephew had said about Sylvia. "But I don't understand. Why? Why would she come here?"

"My objective in coming here has long been achieved. The reason why I remain here instead of returning home, is standing right next to me," she said, smiling at Marcellus.

"So, you're staying here out of love?" Marius just beamed. "Some things just don't change in 2,000 years, right Marcellus?" He punched his nephew on the shoulder. Marius was clearly happy with what he had just learned, being somewhat of romantic himself. He only wished his own wife would show some of this romanticism sometimes.

As if reading his mind, Marcellus said, "I think this secret should not be shared with Valentina."

His uncle just looked at him. "I am sorry, uncle, but I don't think she is trustworthy." Marcellus was basing this on the slight flirtations she had thrown his way, flirtations which created awkward moments when he was forced to parry them. If she could betray her husband in this way, she could betray them.

His uncle looked carefully at him. "I agree," he blandly replied. "Would you mind explaining to me some of the terrible things Gaius will do?"

"He will use Macro, head of the Praetorian Guard, as his executioner. He will reestablish the treason trials. Many more will die than under Tiberius. He will turn his palace into a virtual brothel. Knowledge of the depredations that will go on there will survive the centuries to titillate the dramas 2,000 years from now. He is currently in an incestuous relationship with his sister, Drusilla."

Sylvia didn't miss the horrified look on Marius's face. "I wish that were all, Marius, but there's more. He will invite couples to dinner. He will then choose one of their wives, lead her away to have sex, and return later to comment to everyone, including her husband, on her performance. Finally, historians don't agree on this. They think he may have suggested he intended to make his horse a consul. Again, whether he says this in jest or not is disputed. His reign will finally end under the swords of Macro and others, a little under four years from now."

She looked at Marcellus. "I wish I had never told you the date or where it happens."

Marcellus gave her a fierce look. "You know I have to be there. I have to do my part."

"He is going to die. It doesn't matter if you're there or not." She begged. "You'll probably end up dead yourself."

"It matters to me! He killed my daughter! My only hope is that it is my thrust that will end the bastard's life," he roared.

Marius looked at him, patted his shoulder, and just nodded. *He's my brother's son alright.*

A couple of minutes later, they were alone in the room. She gave Marcellus a few moments to calm down and then changed the subject. "She's after you, you know… Valentina." Sylvia was dangerously calm when she said this.

"I know," he admitted. "In our culture, it would not be a big deal if I slept with her, as long as it did not turn into an affair. My uncle would not be happy but he would accept it as normal between two young, healthy people. But it would cool our relationship, and right now we have a good one with him."

She stared at him intently. "Well, I'm sorry to say it's not that way in my world. If you sleep with her, I would see it as a betrayal. It might even end our relationship. At the very least, it would hurt me terribly."

"I have absolutely no intention of sleeping with her, whether it concerns your culture or mine. I am so deeply in love with you Sylvia, that the thought of being with anyone else is actually repugnant."

She smiled at him. "She has a fat ass, anyway."

They both laughed. He knew Sylvia was as committed to him as he was to her, even if it wasn't true that Valentina's ass was fat.

Time passed and they settled into a routine. Marius was glad to get the help Marcellus provided. Most of the menial work was done by slaves but

Marcellus was very good at dealing with the finances, having successfully run a shop.

Mealtimes at night were usually an enjoyable affair. Marius seemed to enjoy having someone besides just Valentina around. The three of them eventually became very close, Valentina being the exception. Marcellus had to take pains to avoid being alone with her. And she was hostile to Sylvia when the men weren't around. Bedtime was usually lovemaking time for Marcellus and Sylvia. They couldn't seem to get enough of each other.

It was in the afterglow of one such time that Marcellus turned to Sylvia and asked her to tell him more about the Americans. He smiled. "First of all, I want to hear you say in your own language, English, that you love me and will never leave me."

She smiled impishly at him and said in English, "Men can be such assholes. As if this guy doesn't know I love him to death. He could do with bathing a little bit more, but it's all right. He's by far the best lover I've ever had even if he is a little smelly sometimes."

Marcellus smiled broadly. "That sounded so romantic, even if I didn't understand a single word. It did sound a bit like German."

Sylvia laughed aloud. She had a hard time stopping. Marcellus was no dummy. "Okay, what did you really say?" he ruefully asked.

This just set her off on another fit of laughter. "Why I just said you are the best lover that's ever existed and that I love your smell," she answered innocently.

"My smell?"

Which set off another fit of laughter. "Be careful, woman, or I might have to discipline you."

"Ooooh, that sounds like it could be fun," she giggled.

"You're hopeless," he said laughing. "Seriously though, I've heard a lot about your science and technology. What are your people like?"

"Well, most Americans think their country is the best in the world, just like you Romans think the Roman Empire is the end-all and be-all. A lot of people follow a religion called Christianity. It is an ascetic religion. It forbids lovemaking outside of marriage, as an example. I don't think a typical Roman like you would like that. Things have been getting looser on that end, though many still pay lip service to it. Hmmm, let's see. The pace of living is killing. Things move much more slowly here. Oh, and it's very noisy. All these things make people very stressed."

She grew thoughtful. "Go on," he urged.

"There is a lot of crime. A lot of killing. Let's see… We don't even come close to taking care of our families the way you people do. Old people are often put away in institutions."

"Why that's terrible," he said.

"Marcellus, you have to understand. People live much longer in my time. The average person lives into their 80s. Many of them become demented. A family would not be able to take care of a person who could wander off and become lost, or maybe start a fire in the home, just because they were infirm."

"What else?" He prompted.

"This is the part you're going to like. Even though the political entity, the Roman Empire, fell some 1600 years ago, much of your culture still survives and influences our way of life. As an example, many of our laws come down from your time. In my country, we have a Senate, similar to yours. Up until just recently, that religion I told you about, Christianity, performed most of its ceremonies in Latin. Many of our English words have a Latin root. Latin itself is a dead language, but five of our modern languages directly descend from Latin. You would probably be able to get the gist of one of these languages if you heard it spoken. Unfortunately, English is not one of those languages. You once told me it sounded like German. That's not surprising because German and English both have the same root."

"Our medicine is much better than yours. Many diseases that exist now
have been eradicated. Hmmm, let's see… The vast majority of women do
not die in childbirth, nor do their children. Most of them live to grow into
adulthood. And speaking of children, women can avoid pregnancy if they
wish. This has resulted in women getting equal rights to men, at least in
law. There is no job forbidden to women. Some of them even become
soldiers and fight in wars. Now this is my country I'm talking about. Some
countries still do not give women rights."

"You must miss these things terribly," he mused sadly.

"I have you, don't I?"

He just smiled at her. "Then I don't miss anything," she quietly said,
nestling into his arms.

Chapter 21

Ardea   39 CE

The next two years proceeded without incident. The fear that had dominated both of their lives, slowly dissipated. Their uncle Marius was not bothered in the least by their company. If fact, he relished it. The only fly in the ointment was Valentina. It had become pretty obvious to Marcellus and Sylvia that Valentina was indeed a gold digger who had not married out of love, or if there was any love, it was love of money.

Marius, on the other hand, loved her to death. She used this to her advantage. He could not bear the thought of losing the now 27-year-old beauty. She mistreated him terribly, holding the threat of her leaving to her advantage. She spent extravagantly. It was fortunate that the farm was so prosperous or she might have driven it bankrupt. She was very rude and unkind to Sylvia, but was careful to be this way only when alone with her. Sylvia would've loved to be able to practice some of her martial arts on the bitch, but knew that would be impossible.

By far the worst thing was, however, the way she continued to pursue Marcellus. Sylvia was convinced this was just another way for Valentina to get at her. For whatever the reason, Marcellus had to be very careful around her. His uncle had noticed and was saddened by it. The only reason he didn't show his nephew the door was that he had perceived how carefully Marcellus had parried her all of her moves. *She needs a good thrashing,* he often thought about his wayward wife, but he dared not do it lest she leave him. He failed to perceive this was just an idle threat. She would never leave the money and comfortable life Marius provided.

Things came to a head that summer. It had been a beautiful, sunny day. Sylvia was out in the garden tending roses. Marcellus was in his room, changing his tunic from a hard day's work. Valentina appeared in the door with a funny look on her face.

"I've waited long enough," she hissed and started removing her clothing.

"Valentina! Stop! What are you doing?" he asked in great panic.

"What do you think I'm doing?" She sarcastically asked. "It's time you and I got better acquainted."

"But Marius-"

"FUCK MARIUS!" she shouted. "This is going to happen, and it's going to happen NOW! I know you are not homosexual. I've had to hear you and Sylvia night after night, but now it's time I collected my due."

He looked at her in stunned surprise. She looked at him coyly. She had completed removing all of her clothes and approached him sinuously. "Don't you find me attractive?" she cooed.

Marcellus had had enough. "On the outside, you're a very beautiful woman. On the inside, you're a snake," he sneered.

This stopped her dead. She colored deeply and gave him a look of hatred, the likes of which he had rarely seen.

"RAPE!" she screamed. RAPE!" She ran out of the room, screaming that Marcellus had tried to rape her.

Marius made a quick appearance. Marcellus had just exited the room, following Valentina. "Uncle, I-"

"Not another word, Marcellus. I know what's going on here." He turned to his wife. "Such a strange thing, this so-called rape. You are naked. Marcellus is fully-clothed." He considered. "You need to be disciplined, my dear. It is long overdue. Go to our room and wait for me," he sternly demanded.

For the first time in their marriage, she became frightened of him. "But Marius, he-"

"ENOUGH!" he roared. "To our room, NOW, or you can pack your bags and leave."

She hesitated and looked at him. He just pointed to their room. She knew he was serious and slowly did as told.

Marius turned to his nephew. "I apologize for my wife's behavior," was all he said and walked away towards his room.

Just then Sylvia rushed in, having heard the commotion. "What happened?" she asked with some trepidation. She feared some trouble that would end up with them having to leave. Marcellus smiled. "I'll explain later. For now, just listen."

There was a loud commotion coming from Marius's bedroom, lots of shouting and arguing. Then came the indisputable sounds of someone being chastised.

"Oh my God! Is he-"

"Yes indeed," Marius chuckled. "He is, and about time too."

Sylvia just laughed and then said with a smile, "Don't you be getting any ideas."

A few minutes later found Valentina rubbing her burning bottom, while seething, *I'll get that bastard Marcellus back, if it's the last thing I do.*

Later in the day, Sylvia couldn't help smirking and giving her bottom a little rub as she passed Valentina. Of course, that completely infuriated Valentina. She was already humiliated and to be teased on top of that, was simply too much. *You won't be smirking when I'm through with you,* she thought maliciously.

The two of them couldn't help giggling that night in bed about what had happened to Valentina. "I'd say she finally got what she deserved," said Marcellus.

Sylvia sobered a bit. "But she's dangerous, Marcellus. We'd be wise to really watch our backs from here on in. She'll try to find a way to get her revenge."

"I really don't see what she could do," he said. "Uncle is on to her now."

But Marcellus couldn't have been more wrong. A couple of days later found Valentino in her room, busily writing a note:

Valentina hoped to kill two birds with one stone with this note. She was hoping all three, which included her husband, would be arrested, leaving her in possession of the farm. She entrusted the sealed note to the household slave, Rufus, whom she had noticed giving her solicitous looks in the past. She felt she could trust him.

"Rufus, I want you to go to Rome, and at the first Roman garrison you find, give this note to an officer. Make sure it's an officer and not a common soldier. I know I can trust you to do this duty." She looked into his eyes and gave him a smile which seemed to promise things to come.

Rufus couldn't believe his luck. "It will be done, Mistress. I will leave right away." His imagination started to run wild. He had not missed the look she had given him, never understanding he was being manipulated, and that his fantasies would never be realized.

Fortunately for the two fugitives, they were liked by most of the household staff because they had always been treated with respect and kindness by the two. One of Sylvia's maids had seen the exchange between Rufus and Valentina. She reported the incident to Sylvia.

"Mistress, I do not know what is in that note but Rufus left right away for Rome and Valentina seemed excited," said the girl. "That woman is malevolent and I wouldn't put anything past her."

Sylvia went straight to Marcellus with the news. "I know she can be quite the bitch but do you really think she could do something this evil?" He asked.

"Oh, she's capable alright. You don't see how she treats me when you and your uncle aren't around. The only reason she doesn't try to hit me is that she knows I'd beat the snot out of her if she ever tried."

Marcellus looked doubtful. "All right then, just to be safe, let's have some of our bags packed with essentials and money in case we have to run. Marcellus included the gladius and pugio he had taken from that guard so long ago in what he considered essentials. I'm also going to ask Quintus to keep a lookout. He usually works near the gate and we'd at least get a bit of a warning before any soldiers arrived."

It took a few weeks for the news to percolate up to Caligula, but percolate it did. He smiled in anticipation of what he was going to do to those two once he got his hands on them.

Chapter 22

Ardea   39 CE

The order was given. "Arrest them, but do not kill them. I need to meet with them. Caligula smiled in anticipation. *I'm going to enjoy that bitch once and for all before I kill her.*

Marcellus and Sylvia had decided to warn their uncle at what Valentina may have done. He just sighed and shook his head. "Sadly, I know she is capable of this. She was very angry at being punished. I just thought I'd be denied marital privileges for a while, but this wouldn't surprise me."

"Uncle, I am so very sorry to have put you in this position. This is my fault. You should never have had to share in the danger," Marcellus said, shaking his head.

"If she has indeed done this, then the fault is not yours. But let's not jump to conclusions. Maybe there's an innocent reason behind her sending that note to Rome," replied his uncle, hoping beyond hope that Valentina had not done this.

He decided to confront her. "Valentina, what was in the note you sent to Rome?"

She shook her head. She was not prepared for this. She hadn't realized she had been observed. "What note?" she asked.

This answer, plus the fact she looked alarmed, told Marius all he needed to know. "I know you don't love me. I accepted this a long time ago. And I've put up with your childish, boorish behavior for years now. But this." He actually teared up. "But this. I would've thought this was beyond you. That you are not this evil." He stared at her intently. "I should kill you."

She backed up, then quavered, "Marius, I don't know what you're talking about."

"Then what was in that note, Valentina?"

"I don't know what note you're talking about," she insisted.

"For Jupiter's sake, Valentina, you were seen, and I also interrogated Rufus. He didn't know what was in the note but he did know that he was to deliver it to a military officer."

Valentina grew terribly frightened. She tried to run out the doorway. Marius blocked her way. "Yes, I should kill you, but I cannot. You are fortunate. You do not love me, but I love you. Still, if you are wise, you will stay out of my sight. If I see you, I might change my mind."

Later on, Marcellus was trying to convince Marius, "You need to leave with us, uncle. Caligula will not be too happy with you having harbored us."

Marius just shook his head. "This is my land. I am nothing without it. And besides, I am too old to be running. But you two need to leave. As soon as possible."

Marcellus looked thoroughly miserable, and said again, "Uncle, I am so, so sorry."

"And I am not," replied Marius. "These past two years have been a joy, discovering what a fine man I have for a nephew, and what a wonderful woman his wife is."

Sylvia teared up. "And I, Marius, have also discovered what a fine uncle Marcellus has. I shall never forget what you have done for us. I love you as if you were my very own father." She moved forward and hugged him tightly.

Marius, clearly very moved, was without words. He finally choked out, "You two need to leave. Now. Go!"

They parted with heavy hearts. Marcellus and Sylvia went to their room to make final preparations. Marius went and sat in his courtyard. *How could I have made such a mistake as marrying that bitch? Her beauty beguiled me and look what the result is.* He sighed deeply. *I really don't know what to do with her. I cannot kill her. But I think the Emperor, Gaius, will solve that problem for us. She is pretty naïve if she thinks she will escape this unscathed.*

Valentina was both excited and frightened to be in Caligula's palace a month later. Her excitement came from her surroundings. Her room was spacious and well-stocked. She had never experienced a palace so magnificent, so opulent. It made her former residence at Marius's farm seem like a chicken coop in comparison. She had been treated with kindness and courtesy since she had arrived a couple of days ago. She saw this as a good sign for her future prospects. At the very least, she expected to be granted Marius's farm.

Her fear arose from the persona of Caligula himself. She knew he was a dangerous man. Many had died under his reign. She would have to be really careful on how she dealt with him. She had always been confident in her ability to manipulate men. Unfortunately, Marcellus's rebuffs to her repeated attempts at seduction had eroded that confidence somewhat. She was a bit fearful that she wouldn't be up to the challenge.

She was summoned to his quarters the next day. She was not surprised the audience would take place in his bedroom. Caligula's reputation in these matters was well-known.

Caligula looked at her appraisingly. "My goodness, but you are a beautiful woman," was his first comment to her. "I was told you were good looking, but now I find these reports understated you."

This only bolstered her confidence. She bowed to him and said in as an alluring voice as she could manage, "I thank you, Caesar, for your kind words." Again, playing the seductress, she added, "I am your humble servant and your desires shall be my command."

Caligula smiled inwardly. *By Jupiter, that was crudely put. She may be beautiful, but probably has the intelligence of a toad. Still, she has her uses.*

"Valentina, that is your name, right? Valentina?"

"Yes, Caesar."

"You may disrobe."

She was surprised at how quickly and bluntly he had acted. This caused her to hesitate. "Caesar?"

By the gods, she really is dim, he thought, misinterpreting her hesitation.

"Take off your clothes, Valentina. That is what "disrobe" means," he said in a bored voice.

This is not a good start. He must think I'm a country bumpkin, she dejectedly thought. Her worried thoughts caused her to hesitate again.

"By all the gods, Valentina, is there something wrong with your hearing?" he exasperatedly asked. "Take. Off. Your. Clothes."

Being treated like an idiot made her feel like one. She had planned for this moment to be alluring and seductive. Instead, feeling thoroughly embarrassed, she awkwardly removed her tunic.

He sighed, "Your underwear too." He was starting to wonder if this was worth the bother. She rapidly complied.

He patted the bed. "Come and see what your Emperor has for you."

Their lovemaking was both perfunctory and short. "Well that was almost a complete waste of time," he sighed. "You may be beautiful, but you're not very good at this, are you?"

She teared up at the insult. Caligula was probably the worst lover she had ever experienced. He had given her no time to be ready. It had actually hurt a little bit. He had obviously been bored throughout the whole time and he had made no pains to pretend otherwise.

What he said next completely shocked her. "You will become part of my kitchen staff. I hope you are better at preparing food than what you are in bed."

"But Caesar," she wailed.

"Silence!" he commanded. "You are lucky I do not have you put to death. You and your husband harbored criminals for two years."

"Caesar, I implore you. It was my husband, not I, who committed this crime."

Dumb, and loyalty is not one of her virtues, if she even has any. "Well, you need not worry about your husband anymore. He is no longer among the living. Leave me now."

"But Caesar, please-"

"I said, go! If I am forced to repeat this one more time, you will join your husband," he warned.

Valentina left his room dejectedly. All her hopes were dashed. She ruefully regretted having ever written that note.

~~~~~~~~~~~~~~~~~~~~~~~~~~~~~

Marcellus and Sylvia had been hiding in the town of Formiae for the last couple of weeks. They had been too afraid to venture forth as patrols from the Roman garrison at nearby Casinum had started to become much more frequent. Marcellus had been paying a small fortune to this tavern keeper to buy his silence.

"They're obviously looking for us," Marcellus sighed. "Somehow, we have to get out of Italy."

Sylvia looked at him morosely. "It's just a question of time before they find us."

Marcellus was surprised at this. He had never seen her so despondent. "Keep the faith, my love. We're not caught yet."

She looked deeply into his eyes. "Marcellus, we need to split up."

"What!? Why would you even say such foolishness?"
~~~~~~~~~~~~~~~~~~~~~~~~~~~~~

"You'd have a better chance without me, my love. I stand out here. I'm tall. I'm fair skinned. I have flaming red hair. I'm the one who'll get us captured."

"Don't even say that! We've avoided them so far, haven't we?"

"Marcellus, people here notice me. I get looks all the time. You, on the other hand, look like a typical Roman. If I wasn't with you-"

"ENOUGH!" he roared. "I've heard enough of this foolishness!"

She was taken aback by his vehemous reaction. "But-"

"I said, enough," he hissed. "Don't you understand that I'd rather die with you, than live without you?" He placed his hands on both sides of her face. "Without you, I am nothing."

She sighed deeply and the tears began to flow. "I just can't bear the thought that I might cause your death," she sobbed.

"Do not despair, my love. Did you not tell me Gaius only has a little more than a year to live? Surely, we can avoid him that long. We must not lose hope," he urged.

"And then what?" she asked.

"Then, Claudius. Did you not tell me he was a good man? Did you not tell me he was a good Emperor? Does he not end all the killing?"

"Yes," she simply answered. He was looking at her so tenderly that she only sighed, and hugged him fiercely. "I guess we'll have to manage," she whispered.

"We are going to have to leave this place, however. I don't trust the owner and besides, we'll run out of money long before the year is up if we keep paying him these usurious rates."

Chapter 23

Formiae 39 CE

Sylvia nudged Marcellus who was still sleeping. It was 2 AM in the morning. "Marcellus, wake up. It's time."

He gradually woke from his stupor. He yawned. "I guess I fell asleep."

She snorted. "I had to prod you a couple of times to stop your snoring. Anyway, I think it's safe. I haven't heard a single sound in the last hour or so."

They gathered the belongings they had prepared earlier in the day. They tiptoed down the stairs and out the door. Sylvia's heart was beating fast. She did not want to wake the tavern keeper. It was best if he did not know which direction they had gone. The idea was to head east, across Italy. Their ultimate goal was to cross the Adriatic Sea and possibly hide out in Greece. The main problem was they'd have to pass near the Roman garrison at Cassinum.

The first early morning passed without incident. They had decided to only travel when it was dark. Dawn came all too soon for their liking. Marcellus knew it would be better if they were not on the road now. Sylvia had been correct. Their searchers would have an easy time locating them just by inquiring about a tall, redheaded woman, if they traveled by daylight. He spotted an old, abandoned barn. There were a lot of these around lately as the small, middle-class farms were being absorbed by the very wealthy landowners and integrated into huge plantations.

"So, this is where we're supposed to sleep?" Sylvia asked. "I hope the rats don't mind."

He grinned. He found that sometimes she had a strange, humorous way of expressing things. He had never heard the like before and he appreciated it. *Perhaps all people from the future are like this*, he thought. "I suppose the rats will appreciate your beauty as much as I do," he said, playing along. "However, we do need to sleep, and this is our best option."

She looked around at the hay and grinned impishly. "You know, back in my time, we have an expression about taking a tumble in the hay, or something like that anyway. Is that what we're going to do?"

He laughed. "Aren't you afraid of having the rats as an audience?"

"No, not at all. Maybe they'll learn something," she deadpanned.

He roared at this and she found herself giggling at his reaction. And, who knows. Maybe the rats did learn something with what transpired in the next half hour or so. The two of them didn't mind the scratchy hay at all. Afterwards, they slept away the rest of the day.

They awakened a few hours before sunset. Marcellus was getting fidgety about having to wait for the sun to go down. He was anxious to get going. Sylvia, on the other hand, was remarkably patient and calm. *I don't like waiting either,* she thought. *But it's better than the alternative.*

Finally, it was almost dark and they furtively left the barn. Then their luck ran out. Two soldiers had noticed them leaving the barn. As it turns out, they were not specifically looking for the two fugitives. They had just found it a little bit suspicious that Marcellus was wearing a gladius. *Damn,* thought Marcellus, *we should've waited 10 minutes more*. They approached Sylvia and Marcellus.

Marcellus examined them closely as they were nearing. Their demeanor was not right. It looked to him that they had never been in combat. They weren't covering each other and they were looking at Sylvia as much as him, which is not what an experienced soldier would do.

He quickly ascertained which one of the two was the most dangerous. He made no move until that soldier was close enough and then he quickly lashed out with all his might to the soldier's face. That one fell to the ground, momentarily stunned at the unexpected attack. The other one managed to pull his gladius out, but not as quickly as Marcellus who slashed him at the knee. He slashed at Marcellus before going down writhing and screaming in agony.

Marcellus quickly turned to the other one who had not regained all of his senses. He moved on him, obviously intending to thrust his gladius into the soldier's stomach.

"MARCELLUS, NO!" screamed Sylvia.

He turned to her. "Damn your timeline. This one is dangerous to us."

"It's not just the timeline. You don't have to kill him now. It wouldn't be right."

"He'll report us," seethed Marcellus.

"Yes, but if you sever his Achilles instead," she looked at the other one, "and this one's also. We'll have a few hours head start before they're discovered. They won't be able to walk if you do this."

"Achilles?"

"The tendon at the back of the ankle."

He didn't know what a tendon was but he understood the injury she wanted him to inflict. "If we let them live, they'll still report us," he argued. He had been a soldier. He would have no problem killing someone who was a danger to him.

"Yes, Marcellus, but I don't think I could live with myself if we kill them. They are helpless now."

He looked at her and then looked at them. They were demonstrating pathetic pleading looks which the soldier in him despised. A true Roman soldier should face death more bravely. He sighed. "This is a mistake," he said, and then slashed both of their ankles.

"You should thank the lady for your lives," he said disdainfully. They only moaned in pain. The two hurried off down the road. "We will have to make haste now before they are discovered," he warned. "And then, we're going to have the whole damn garrison after us."

Marcellus found himself warring with the mixed feelings inside of him. He was pleased to have a wife who was so kindhearted. But he was also angry at her for stopping him from doing what he knew he should have done.

"Marcellus, you're bleeding!" Sylvia gasped.

"It's just a scratch," he assured her.

She looked carefully at his arm just below the shoulder. "That's no scratch," she admonished. "It's bleeding a lot for just a scratch. You're going to need stitches." She was grateful it wasn't a wound typical in modern warfare. There would be no need to extract a bullet.

"Stitches?"

"I'm going to have to sew the wound closed," she explained.

"Ah," he said. "I am familiar with this. But we have no time to do this now." He tore a strip from his tunic. "Bind this tightly around the wound. When we have gotten far enough away, Sylvia, you will be able to sew your 'stitches'."

A little time passed and Sylvia noticed that Marcellus had slowed down a bit. No doubt the blood loss was starting to have an effect. "We need to find a place to stop," she said.

"I agree. I was thinking we should get off this road and head northeast for Sora. The garrison at Cassinum will be expecting us to go either east or west on the main road, not northeast."

"Alright, you know better than me. Sounds good."

"There's a problem with this however, Sylvia. My idea is to continue in this direction until we reach the Via Tibertuna. Even though the Via Tibertuna starts in Rome, we will be quite a distance from there when we join it. This road will lead to the East Coast and the town called Aternum." He sighed. "The problem is we would have to cross the Apennines first, going this way. I'm not even sure if there's any trail or path that does this."

"And I don't even have my hiking boots," she joked.

He frowned. He didn't quite understand what she had said. Sometimes Marcellus got confused when Sylvia joked, not realizing that she was joking.

"Anyway," he continued. "At the very least, we can hide out at Sola. I'm pretty certain the garrison commander would never consider it as our destination as it leads into the Apennines."

It took the most of the night to reach the vicinity of Sola. She worried about Marcellus. He was pretty white faced and it was obvious he was struggling. "There," she pointed. "There's an old shack. It looks deserted."

"Looks more like an outhouse," Marcellus grumbled.

"Beggars can't be choosers," she replied.

He thought about what she had just said, and then realizing, just grinned. "No, I guess not."

The shack was not an outhouse, which made Sylvia very grateful. But it was in pretty bad shape. Still, it was shelter, even if it did have a big hole in the roof near the far wall. They were forced to sit on the floor. Once they were settled, she pulled out her medical kit. There was a needle and surgical thread. She thanked Tegar Industries for having prepared for every emergency and was satisfied at herself for being smart enough to hang onto the kit all this time.

"This is going to hurt." She unbound his arm and applied some rubbing alcohol. He didn't understand why, but he had learned over the years that Sylvia was better than any doctor he had ever experienced. She began to sew. She wasn't surprised that Marcellus didn't make a peep. He only grimaced. She already knew how tough her old soldier was.

When she had finished, he said, "Sylvia, now you have to gather some wood and start a fire."

"Why?" she asked perplexed. "It's pretty warm out."

"You need to heat my gladius and place it over my wound. This will prevent any 'soldier's sickness' later on."

"Thank God there is no need for that, Marcellus." She slabbed on copious amounts of antibiotic cream. Then she pulled two pills out of her kit. "Swallow these pills, and you will not get any infection, as long as you keep taking these pills for the next little while." Next, she bound his wound tightly with bandages from the kit. *I should've done this earlier. I'm not happy with that strip of tunic we used. It couldn't have been very hygienic. But we were just in such a hurry and in such a panic. Still, I should've stopped and applied the proper bandages.*

He looked at her. "I am grateful for the miracles of your time," he simply said. They were both exhausted and slept most of the day.

Chapter 24

Sola 39 CE

They ended up staying in Sola for the next couple of months. Marcellus
was correct in thinking the soldiers would not be searching there. The town
was tiny and the two of them couldn't help being noticed. The townspeople
pretty much realized they must be fugitives because Marcellus was
wounded, and they didn't seem to have any real reason for coming here.
Fortunately, the townspeople had never been fond of Rome. As a matter of
fact, they had allied themselves with Hannibal when he was devastating
Italy in the second Punic war. So they were more than glad to offer the pair
sanctuary. Still, Marcellus figured they had to eventually leave. It was too
close to the garrison at Cassinum, and it was only a matter of time before
the news trickled out that there were two fugitives here.

Marcellus's wound had mostly healed without any problems. One day, she
noticed him staring at her strangely. "What?" she asked.

"You once told me women of your time had a way of preventing pregnancy.
Is that what you're doing now?"

"No. Too much time has passed for me to use most of these methods
which required modern technology. There is one method that would've
worked over this long period of time, but it would've required a doctor to
implant it. And it wouldn't have been very hygienic not to keep changing
these implants."

"Then why are you not getting pregnant? Are you too old?"

She laughed. "Give me a break. I'm only 33."

"Then why?"

"I have no idea." She smiled at him. "There certainly have been numerous
opportunities for me to get pregnant."

He smiled back.

She continued, "It could be the stress we've been living under. It could be what happened to Livia. Really, I don't have a clue. I think it's best right now that I don't get pregnant. Think of how difficult things would be if we had to take care of a baby now. But, Marcellus, we only have to last a little over a year more. Once Gaius is gone, I would be more than happy to have your children." She gave him a slightly amused look. "And I won't be too old for that to happen."

Vitus finally reported the news that was inevitable. The garrison at Cassinum had learned of two fugitives held up in Sola. Four soldiers had been dispatched to investigate. But Marcellus and Sylvia had not wasted their time in Sola. They had prepared as well as they could for mountain hiking and they had procured the services of a guide, Septimus Lucius, an expert on mountaineering. They were ready to go at a moment's notice.

Septimus arrived at their temporary lodging before they had a chance to summon him. "Time to go," was all he said. At first, traveling was easy. They only had to deal with foothills, and the weather remained pleasant for this late fall time. That ended too soon, as far as Sylvia was concerned. The going started to get more difficult, and it got colder the further they went. Progress slowed down also.

"My legs are just killing me," Sylvia complained at one point.

"We can stop and make camp here," Septimus offered. He was often very solicitous as far as Sylvia was concerned. It was quite obvious he was very fond of her. Sylvia, herself, was embarrassed. Sure, it had been years since her training with Tegar Industries, but she felt she should be doing better than this. Marcellus usually could go further than Sylvia, but he was very understanding. He did not want to tax her more than what she could take. He understood that when she admitted she was tired, she was actually nearing the end of her ability to go on.

It went on like this for about a week until they encountered a wooden bridge with no handrails. The drop down looked to be over a thousand feet. Marcellus gasped. "My balance has never been very good. Is there no other way around this?" he asked, already knowing the answer.

"No, I'm afraid not," Septimus offered. "Sylvia, is this going to be a problem for you also?"

She looked down. "No, not really. My balance is good and I'm not afraid of heights." She doubted she would've qualified for Tegar Industries if this were not true.

"Alright," Septimus said. "Some people say it's best for the frightened one to go hand-in-hand with the experienced one." (Marcellus despised the terminology "frightened one"). "But I have found that usually ends up with two plunging down into the depths, instead of just one. So here is what we are going to do. Sylvia and I will cross first. Marcellus, you will get down on your hands and knees and crawl across the bridge. Make sure you don't look down as you do so and try to ignore any swaying you should happen to feel."

"You want me to crawl," Marcellus asked indignantly. Sylvia had to stifle a laugh.

"If you have a better idea, I'm all ears," replied Septimus. "I'm afraid you'll have to swallow your pride. It's the safest way. And I've never lost a single soul using this technique." Septimus knew he and Sylvia had to go first. Otherwise, the frightened one might not even try. But they always did try when their companions were already on the other side. He hoped the crawling one wouldn't freeze somewhere in the middle as they often did, and have to be coaxed into continuing.

It usually took about a minute to cross the bridge. It took Marcellus 10 minutes. He did exactly as he was told, feeling thoroughly embarrassed as he did so. He was not accustomed to acting in what he considered a shameful way in the face of danger. Any swaying of the bridge invariably ended up with him hugging it tightly as if his life depended on it. Sylvia felt sympathy for him. She knew he was terrified and ashamed all at the same time. Once across the bridge, nobody said anything for a little while. They all thought it was for the better.

It took a full month to cross the Apennines. "We made pretty good time," offered Septimus. "And that's a good thing because winter is coming on. I don't think I would've even attempted this in the winter. You two have no experience with mountain hiking when there is snow. It is 10 times more dangerous then.

"Well, I'd better be heading home. I am probably going to have to deal with a little bit of winter before I make it back." Marcellus reached into his pouch and gave Septimus an aurea.

"What is this for? he asked. "You already paid."

"Yes," said Marcellus. "But after having experienced this trip and knowing you have to repeat it, maybe even in winter conditions, I realize you were underpaid."

"I assure you this is unnecessary." Septimus had grown very fond of the two.

"I insist," said Marcellus. Septimus accepted it reluctantly.

"Follow that trail for about 10 miles and you will come to the Via Tibertuna. I believe none of your pursuers will expect to find you there. You should be safe for the rest of your expedition. The three hugged closely and then split apart for their respective journeys.

The trip to Aternum was uneventful. Aternum was an important seaport on the Adriatic Sea. Both the Via Tibertuna and the coastal Via Adriatica ran through it. Its harbor was used for military purposes, besides commercial ones. It was an important Roman gateway to the eastern part of the Empire.

"I don't think they'll be looking for us here, seeing as the garrison at Cassinum reported a sighting down there in the south. They'll be focusing their search on Formia if they think we'll try the Tyrrhenian Sea, or Histonium, if they think were planning to escape by the Adriatic Sea. Both of those places are much further south. And besides, I don't think the search for us is a priority. Gaius certainly would like to get his hands on us, but I don't believe he's desperate to do so."

He sighed. "Just the same, I think we should change our names. And for you my love, we need to make a more radical change. We should cut your hair short and dye it brown. You should wear loose-fitting male clothes. And maybe wear a hood. We'll make up some excuse like you have an injury on your head that you're shy about. I'll try to pass you off as my teenage son."

"Why all the changes, all of a sudden?" she asked, somewhat surprised.

"Because I don't think we'll be able to secure passage across the Adriatic right now. It's winter, and even if we could, it would be more dangerous than what I feel comfortable with. So, we'll need to stay in Aternum for a little while, at least till Spring. "Let's see, hmmm, I'm Pontius, and you're-"

"Adrianus," she interrupted. "I've always loved the name Adriana."

It was not difficult to find the black-market people willing and able to make the necessary changes on Sylvia. Marcellus always looked sternly at each of those who had done so. "If I even hear a rumor about changes made to an attractive female, I will return here, and you will join the gods in the heavens." Each took him seriously. Marcellus looked formidable. Even if they thought they could take him, why risk the bother. Besides, silence was part of their tradecraft.

Marcellus managed to rent a comfortable apartment at a decent rate. A few months passed uneventfully. His neighbors couldn't help but like Marcellus, with his outgoing, friendly behavior. They did find his son a little bit strange though. He was unusually tall while his father wasn't. He rarely spoke, and when he did, his voice was unnaturally high. He always wore that stupid hood. And he never went to the public baths. Many thought Pontius must have adopted him.

Aternum was an interesting town. It had a public bath like most Roman towns. It had a surprisingly large number of temples for a town that size. The most impressive one was the temple of Jovis Aternum. Marcellus believed the town must be wealthy to be able to build such a fine temple. Finally, there was the magnificent bridge over the Aternius Fluvius, built by Tiberius. *He must've believed this town was going to grow much larger to build such a big bridge,* mused Marcellus.

Chapter 25

Aternum 40 CE

It was late Spring. "I think we have dawdled here long enough. I know it feels safe and it's certainly very comfortable, but I don't want to push our luck," worried Marcellus.

"There is another reason to leave, my love," Sylvia said, smiling at him.

He gave her a quizzical look.

"I am pregnant, at least three months."

He gasped, and stared at her in shock, eyes very wide open. Then he took her in his arms. Both were joyful and started laughing.

"Your neighbors already think I'm pretty strange. What will they think when I start showing?"

He guffawed at that. He just loved her wit. He always had. "You may have a point," he finally managed through his laughter.

It ended up taking over a month to arrange passage over the Adriatic Sea. They decided, in the interests of safety, not to inform their neighbors of their leaving. They planned to slip away in the middle of the night. This strategy saved their lives. They were not expected to show up at the harbor in the middle of the night, and when they did, an unpleasant surprise awaited them. Soldiers from the local garrison were stealthily taking up positions.

"That bastard of a captain must have betrayed us. It is only pure, dumb luck that we decided at the last moment to come here now instead of the morning. Someday that man will pay," swore Marcellus wrathfully. "What really angers me is that I already advanced him a full Auria, something we can't really afford. We do not have much left."

Sylvia remained cool. "We need to go back to our apartment, but we can't remain too long. It's only a question of time before they realize we're not going to show up at the boat, and they make their way here."

They were very surprised to find their neighbor and good friend, Antonius, making his way quickly out of his own apartment. "What happened? Why are you back here?"

"What do you mean?" asked Marcellus.

"I thought you and your wife were finally making your escape."

"My wife?" responded a surprise Marcellus.

Antonius just laughed. "You may have fooled everyone else, but I have a nose for beautiful women. And your wife is a beautiful woman despite all your efforts to hide this."

Sylvia grinned ruefully. "I thank you, I think."

"Soldiers were waiting for us at the harbor. That son of a bitch captain must've betrayed us."

"Well, it certainly isn't safe for you here. I have a small hunter's cabin just a few miles out of town. You can hide there for the time being if you want." Antonius considered some more. "I've come to know you two very well. You are not criminals. So why is that bastard Gaius after you?"

"He tried to rape Sylvia. That is her real name by the way. Anyway, he tried to rape her years ago, before he became emperor. I struck him. What really angered him, is that Tiberius refused to punish me, as he pretty much figured out what had transpired. He's hated us from that moment. We knew we had to run the moment he was made Emperor."

Antonius just sighed. "Our dear Emperor is not one to forgive and forget. If he catches you, you're both dead. So what say you? My cabin?"

Marcellus grasped Antonius's arm. "You are a true friend. I don't know if we can risk your life this way."

"What choice do you have? You think I don't understand the risks? You two are worth it," he said earnestly.

Tears came to Sylvia's eyes. "We will be in your eternal debt. We will never be able to thank you enough."

Marcellus understood she had made the decision for both of them. He had always considered her his equal, so he accepted that the decision had been made. Sylvia was on the verge of becoming a mother again. At this point, he didn't realize her decision had been made mostly for the benefit of her unborn child.

Summer slowly faded into autumn. Antonius made weekly visits to the cabin, bringing food and reports on what was going on in Aternum. "They seem to have given up searching for you. They went crazy the first couple of weeks after you left. Soldiers were everywhere. They even increased the reward. Fortunately, no one knows about this cabin of mine."

But he was wrong. Someone did know. One of their old neighbors, Vitus knew, and there was nothing Vitus liked better than money. He knew Antonius had been very close to the two fugitives, and he found it suspicious that he disappeared every week with a bunch of supplies. He reported to the Roman commander. He suggested that they tail Antonius when he left on one of his trips.

"If they are found there, do I get the reward?" he asked.

The commander looked at him disdainfully. "Yes," he blandly replied.

"Soldiers!" Marcellus urgently whispered.

"Shit! How did they find out?" Antonius complained. "You need to run! Quickly!" he urged.

"There'll be no running, Antonius. Sylvia's five months pregnant."

They were quickly captured and bound. Sylvia and Marcellus were eventually put on the road to Rome with a guard detail of five soldiers. Antonius was brought before the commander of the garrison.

"So, Antonius, you were harboring fugitives."

Antonius knew where this was going, knew that he was as good as dead. "They are my friends," he calmly replied.

"They are criminals and enemies of the Roman state."

"They are not criminals. We both know who the real criminal is here."

The commander sighed. He knew that Caligula was a bit unhinged. Nevertheless, he needed to act, and act decisively or his inaction would be noticed, with consequences for him. "I should have you crucified as an example to the enemies of Rome. However, in your case, I have decided that your death should be quick."

He turned to one of the guards. "Take this man outside, and behead him."

Once again, Sylvia and Marcellus found themselves bound and half dragged on the road to Rome. Marcellus had begged the leader of the guard detail, Quintilius, to allow Sylvia to ride in the small cart they had brought along with them for provisions, but his plea fell on deaf ears.

"She's pregnant," he had pleaded.

"And that concerns me, how?" the guard had sneered.

The inevitable happened four days into their journey. Sylvia started to complain about severe cramping. This progressed to abdominal pain. Finally, she started to bleed copiously. Her pregnancy ended at five months with what is now called a late miscarriage.

Marcellus turned to the leader of the guards. "You are a dead man," he hissed. He then addressed the rest of them. "And if she dies, you are all dead men."

A couple of them snickered, but some became a bit wary. Marcellus was a formidable man, a former soldier. They would like to have been able to kill him then and there while he was in this vulnerable position. But they had strict orders to deliver the two of them alive. This probably had a lot to do with their decision to finally allow Sylvia to ride in the cart. She probably would've died had they forced her to continue walking.

Sylvia was in a state of profound depression. First, they had killed her precious Livia. And now, they had ended the potential life of another child. At first, she just wanted to die. Later, she considered going back to her time. But even in her depression, she doubted she would be able to leave Marcellus, such was her love for him. She fully recognized that if she remained here, she was probably going to be executed. She could save her life by going back. But what kind of life would it be without Marcellus. If her fate was to die here, at least she would die with him.

Progress was purposely slow. They were afraid Sylvia would die if they proceeded at a normal pace. They finally arrived in Rome a little over a week later.

Chapter 26

Rome late 40 CE

Upon arrival, they separated Marcellus and Sylvia. If he was going to do anything, Marcellus knew he had to get free now. Incongruously, three of the guards went with Sylvia and only two with Marcellus. *They're probably taking her directly to Gaius,* he thought. *Looks better for them if there's three with her. Gaius will naturally assume there was also three guards for me.*

Good thing these guys aren't very good. They unshackled my leg chains once Sylvia was gone, to make better progress. A mistake I never would've made. Proof that my strategy of acting mostly docile is working. Well, here goes.

"You guys are pathetic. Where were you trained? The local food market? I shouldn't be making your job easier, but these ties at my wrist are coming loose. Good thing I'm a fellow soldier and don't want to see you get in trouble." Marcellus hoped they would be dumb enough to buy this ruse.

One approached him to look. Marcellus quickly raised his arms over the unfortunate's head and came down on the other side with a solid choke hold. The other soldier started to advance.

"Back off," Marcellus shouted. "One strong twist of his neck and he's dead." This was quite a gamble. He knew they were under orders not to kill him. Were the two guards friends? These were two things in his favor if it was so.

"I know you are under orders not to kill me. I do not know if you care enough about this one to save his life. What I do know is that if you do not take out your pugio and cut these binds in the next 10 seconds, your friend is dead. And you will have a hard time restraining me, being alone, and not allowed to kill me.

The other guard considered. He was the one who had wished they would've killed Marcellus earlier when he was most vulnerable. He had known something like this could happen. Still, the bastard's wife was still alive. He had said he would only kill them all if she died. Only the commander was at risk because of the miscarriage. Still, he figured it was worth at least one bluff.

He pulled out his pugio. "I can disable you without killing you," he warned.

"That is undoubtedly true. The problem is, your friend here will then be dead. Of that, I guarantee."

Damn, he's right. But we'll be whipped at the very least if he gets away.

Almost as if Marcellus was reading his thoughts, he said, "I know you will be punished, but at least you both will be alive. You can say that you were attacked by a bunch of my friends who managed to get me free. You will still be punished, but maybe it will be less severe if they believe your story." He turned his attention to his captive who was starting to struggle. Any more of that, and I will break your neck." That stopped the struggling.

The other guard considered, and then hung his head. Marcellus knew he had won. "Now, come here, and cut these bonds. Slowly. No wrong moves, or he's dead."

The soldier did as he was told. Marcellus was free. "Now, place your gladius on the ground. That's it." He took the captive's gladius. "I am going to release your friend. I am now armed. I think I could take you both, anyway, if you try anything. But why would you try, when you know you're under orders not to kill me. That surely is a handicap you could not overcome. And one more thing, tell Quintilius that fortune shines on him today because he was not here. I have unfinished business with him.

Marcellus pushed the one he had been holding to the ground. Then he slowly backed away, keeping his eyes on them. Even though he knew they wouldn't pursue, he turned and took off running.

Shortly after these events had taken place, Sylvia was brought before Caligula. He smiled wickedly at her. She glared at him defiantly. "So we meet again," he said in an amused voice. "Only this time, there is no Tiberius to save your pretty ass. I am finally going to enjoy what I should have these many years past. Maybe, it's even better this way. Absence makes the heart grow fonder, and all that."

Sylvia felt she had nothing to lose. *I am going to die so what difference if I die now?* She addressed Caligula haughtily. "You're a joke, you know. The Roman Empire will last another 300 years and have over 70 emperors. You will be known as the worst one. And that's saying a lot because there were many pretty bad ones. You wanted a horse to be a consul. Really? And here's the kicker. If you ask anyone in the future who was Gaius Germanicus Caesar, they wouldn't have a clue. You have become known for all time as Caligula. Everyone's heard about Caligula." She knew he hated that name. She was tempted, but resisted telling him he was less than a month away from dying. She was afraid he would beef up his guards if she did tell.

Caligula was taken aback by her outburst and turned a deep red, but made no move towards her. *How can she know these things? Tiberius claimed she knew the future, but how is this possible?*

What is he waiting for? she glumly thought.

They stared at each other for a few moments. He slowly managed to compose himself. "I expect you're wondering what we're waiting for. Well, we're waiting for a special guest. We want to have your beloved Marcellus watch the entire thing. Don't you think that will be delicious?" he laughed.

They waited some more. Finally, a guard came in and whispered into Caligula's ear. Caligula grew very angry. "What!" he shouted. "May all the gods curse him," he seethed. He turned to Sylvia. "I believe we shall do this on a different day. Take her away."

Sylvia started to worry as she was led away. *Is Marcellus dead? No, he isn't. That bastard would've raped me then and there if Marcellus was dead. There are only two possibilities. One, he is too wounded to watch, so I have to wait until he either recovers or dies before Caligula rapes me. Or, and I so hope this is the case, he has somehow managed to escape. Oh darling, if this is so, run far away. Do not try to rescue me.* But she knew in her heart, this was a forlorn hope.

A few days later, the object of her affection was waiting outside a favorite tavern for soldiers, the Beatus Caupona, located on the Vicus Longus. He had been following Quintilius the last few hours, waiting for a chance to get him alone. Finally, the opportunity presented itself, as Quintilius exited the tavern on his own. It was late and the street was deserted.

Marcellus snuck up on him and grabbed him into a headlock from behind. He held his pugio up to his throat. "And now you pay, you bastard, for the death of my child, as I promised."

"So I am to die without a fair fight?" sneered Quintilius.

Marcellus snorted. "Now why would I do that? Fair fight? You must be insane. This is not a fight for honor. This is an execution of a murderous bastard."

"You, yourself, were a soldier. Orders are orders. I was just doing my duty," he gasped.

"Yes, delivering us to Rome was your duty. Not allowing a woman who was five months pregnant to ride in a cart, that was not your duty. That was the will of a coldhearted bastard. I told you, you would pay. You should've listened."

Marcellus gashed Quintilius's throat. The blood splattered out. Quintilius tried to say something but was not able. The last thing he saw was Marcellus's sneer as his world faded to black. His body was found the next morning.

By midafternoon, the whole barracks was buzzing with the news. Vitus was clearly quite frightened. "Do you think he's going to come after us? He said he'd kill us if his woman died. And that bastard is really strong. I had no doubt he would've been able to break my neck had you not acted the way he wanted."

"Far as I know, she's still alive," replied Octavius.

"Yeah, as far as you know. But you have to know what the Emperor Gaius's going to do to her."

"That may be. But we put her in the cart. We treated her well from then on. She arrived here alive. If he's at all reasonable, he should know we were only following our orders. What else were we supposed to do?"

"I guess it all depends on what he considers our culpability. I know one thing. I'm not leaving this garrison until they find that crazy son of a bitch."

Eventually, Marcellus had snuck up to his old wine shop. Not surprisingly, there were plenty of soldiers about. *They must think I'm addled if they believe I would try to make contact here.* His hiding place proved to be a good vantage point. He was not visible to the soldiers, but he could see into his old shop quite clearly. He was pleased to see Marcipor was still running things. The business looked prosperous. He was surprised and pleased to see a very good-looking woman helping Marcipor. The subtle shows of affection between the two had Marcellus believing Marcipor had taken a wife. *He is a good man and he deserves to be happy,* were his only thoughts as he carefully slinked away.

Chapter 27

Rome 41 CE

Sylvia was fraught with worry. As long as she wasn't being summoned to be raped by Caligula, she figured Marcellus must still be alive. *That sick bastard wants Marcellus to watch as I'm being raped. He doesn't realize this is giving me hope. He's given me a way to know if he's still alive. Hang on, my lover, that sick fuck only has a couple more weeks to live.*

She was being kept in a sparsely furnished room. At least it wasn't a cell, and it was pretty clean by the standards of the day. And she was being treated pretty well by Alba who was functioning as sort of a handmaiden. Alba was always respectful and polite, unlike the guard who had also been assigned to her. Alba had barely spoken to Sylvia the first couple of weeks, but then slowly started to engage in conversation with her. Alba was an older lady, perhaps in her 50s, and she started to assume a motherly role. Sylvia found this immensely amusing, but she was careful to go along with it, and not hurt Alba's feelings.

One day, Alba asked, "What I don't understand, Mistress, is why you're being held here. What did you do?"

"I refused to be raped by our dearly beloved Emperor," Sylvia wryly answered.

Alba worriedly looked around. "Shhh, Mistress, do not say such things aloud."

Sylvia just smiled. "Alba, I can't get into any deeper trouble than what I'm already in. My future is to be raped in front of my husband, and then killed."

Alba gasped. "By all the gods, that is horrible!" She then whispered, "I have heard such things about the Emperor, too many to doubt them. I'm really fortunate not to be in his direct service."

Sylvia gazed at the older woman. She didn't want to get her in trouble. She felt she needed to be more careful in future, regarding her comments about Caligula.

"But you are not in despair. You always look hopeful. I don't understand this," Alba commented.

"That bastard doesn't have long to live."

"Who?" Alba asked.

"Gaius Germanicus Caesar, that's who."

Alba looked at Sylvia in amazement. She had heard the rumors about this woman, that she could see into the future. "How- how do you know this?" she stammered.

Sylvia just sighed. *What to tell her? Ah, what harm can it do? The worst thing would be she would think I'm crazy.* "Alba, you're going to find what I have to say next very hard to believe, but I assure you, it is the absolute truth."

She sighed more deeply. "I am from the far, far future. Two thousand years in the future, to be more precise. Everything that is happening now, is actually ancient history to me, just like the Egypt of the early pharaohs is ancient history to you. I know almost exactly when our monster of an Emperor is going to die, and as I already said, it's a little over two weeks from now."

Her voice took on an urgency. "Listen carefully to me, Alba. You must not say a word of what I have revealed to you. They would probably think you're part of a conspiracy. Also, try to be absent from the palace two weeks from now. There is controversy in my time about the exact date of the assassination. Best to be away from two weeks on until you hear news of the event. There will be a lot of killing going on when it happens. The perpetrators will go on a rampage. Only Claudius will be spared, and he will end up becoming the next Emperor."

Alba was shocked at what she was hearing. She briefly wondered if Sylvia was insane, but quickly discounted that thought. She knew her well enough to know this was not so. Also, Alba had a knack for knowing when people were lying to her. As far as she was concerned, hard as it was to believe, Sylvia spoke truth.

"Then- then why are you here?"

"Oh my God, that's a long story, and one for another day. Suffice it to say the reason became irrelevant after I met Marcellus. I should've left here long ago, but I will never leave here now."

Alba just grinned at her. "I guess the power of love hasn't changed in 2,000 years."

This saddened Sylvia a bit. It reminded her of the time Marius had said almost the exact same thing.

Alba then took on a fierce look. "I will do everything in my power to keep you alive the next couple of weeks, Mistress."

Sylvia was moved by the sentiment. She knew Alba wouldn't actually be able to do much, but that wasn't the point. In the short time the two women had known each other, they had become close.

"Alba! You. Are. To. Make. Yourself. Scarce… after the next couple of weeks. Do you understand me?"

"But-"

"No buts," she shouted, loudly enough for the guard to open the door.

"What's going on here?" he snarled.

Both women looked up in surprise, and both said at the same time, "Nothing!" They looked at each other and chuckled a bit.

The guard just sneered, "Women!" and exited, slamming the door, which set the two of them off giggling.

Sylvia grew serious again. "Do I have your word, Alba?"

After a long moment, Alba nodded reluctantly.

~~~~~~~~~~~~~~~~~~~~~~~~~~~~~~~~~~~~
~~~~~~~~~~~~~~~~~~~~~~~~~~~~~~~~~~~~

It had been difficult for Marcellus to make contact with Cassius Chaerea, the head of the Praetorian Guard, and the leader of the conspiracy against Caligula. He finally learned that the man liked to frequent the Bibe Epulare Caupona, on Via Flaminius. Marcellus just didn't know when. He finally decided to spend a few hours there and just wait for the man to show up. This was a bit risky, staying at a public place for an extended period of time, when he was being sought by Caligula. But time was short. The assassination of Caligula was only a few days away.

His patience paid off as Chaerea finally showed up. Marcellus was hopeful that his sobriety was in the same good shape as his patience had been. It wouldn't do any good if he came across as a drunken oaf. Chaerea was sitting at a table on the other side of the room with two of his companions. Marcellus walked up to them. "May I join you gentlemen?" he politely asked.

The three looked at him with undisguised hostility. "And who the fuck are you?" asked Chaerea.

"Someone who would like to join you in your venture." This caused a great deal of consternation between the three, and one of them started to get up, retrieving his pugio. Marcellus had anticipated this. "And how are you, Marcus Vinicius?" he said, and then turned to the other, "And you, Lucius Annius Vinicianus?"

This stopped them dead and made them wary. "What venture are you talking about?" asked Chaerea. He wanted to make sure this stranger actually knew about the conspiracy.

"A venture that is long overdue. A venture to remove some vermin from our great city."

Alright, so he knows. Is he a spy from Gaius? And what difference would it make if he is. If Gaius suspects us, we're done anyway. "And why do you wish to join us?" asked Chaerea, somewhat intrigued.

"Because that pimple on a pig's ass tried to rape my wife, and when he couldn't, he killed my child. He also was responsible for the death of another one of my children, an unborn child."

"What is your name, stranger?" one of the others asked.

"Marcellus Pontius Silanus."

"Alright, Marcellus Pontius Silanus. We'll check you out and let you know in a week or so what we decided," offered Chaerea.

Marcellus laughed. "Nice try, Chaerea. You are planning to kill him in the next three or five days. I'm not sure which. The plan is to wait for him to be alone in the tunnel under the palace and dispatch him there."

The three were shocked. "Chaerea, we need to kill this guy. I don't know how he came by this knowledge, but it is a danger to us," hissed Vinicius.

"You don't trust me. You think maybe Gaius sent me. But why would he do this? If he already knew, he wouldn't send a solitary agent to confront you. He would send a battalion and you probably would already be dead. And I am a soldier who vowed revenge on that prick. I fought in the German campaigns and there is no death that will give me greater satisfaction than this one."

He gazed intently at Chaerea. "You are angry because he makes fun of you, always making derogatory remarks. And you two are probably upset about his plans to move the capital to Egypt. And members of the Senate are paying all three of you. But who has more reason than me? Who has lost children? Who has had his wife assaulted?"

The three looked at each other and said nothing for a few minutes. Finally, Chaerea said simply, "Meet us here in the early morning in three days time. We will trust you, Marcellus Pontius Silanus, but if you try to betray us, your life won't be worth shit."

Marcellus just smiled. "I'll be there. May we succeed in our venture."

The fatal day finally arrived. The three assassins were patiently waiting in the tunnel for Caligula to arrive. They tensed as a figure approached. But it wasn't Caligula. It was Marcellus.

"By all the gods, what are you doing here?" Chaerea angrily asked.

"I had a feeling you guys might try this. So, when you didn't show up at that café, I figured I should head straight here. You forget, I knew exactly where you would be. And if you weren't here today, you'd be here in two days time," Marcellus smugly replied.

"And how did you get the guards to allow you in here?" Although Chaerea had a good idea, as Marcellus was dressed in the garb of a Praetorian Guard.

Marcellus laughed. "Your security is an absolute joke. I told your guards that I was new, and that you, Chaerea, had ordered me to join you here to gain some experience. I fully expected this not to work and was prepared to attack the two guards. But, surprise, surprise, the ruse worked. It certainly shouldn't have. I think the festive atmosphere of the games going on and the supposed lack of any real danger, led to this negligence. Plus, I knew the name of Chaerea. One of the guards actually wished me luck."

The three looked at him in dismay. "If you do anything to ruin our plans, I'll kill you. I hope you realize this," Chaerea warned.

"I don't understand why you can't believe that I want Gaius dead more than you do," a frustrated Marcellus responded.

Vinicius drew his gladius. "We should kill him," he snarled.

Chaerea stepped in front of Vinicius. "Stop," he commanded. "Marcellus, if you could excuse us for a couple of minutes." He started to walk away, to get out of Marcellus's earshot. He beckoned his men to follow.

"If we try to kill him, he'll fight. The ensuing ruckus will be noticed. Our plans will be ruined. I'm afraid we don't have a choice. We have to let him participate and hope he doesn't do anything, purposely or not, to screw our enterprise." Chaerea could tell that they didn't like it, but they didn't have a viable option.

They returned to Marcellus. "Alright, you can stay. Just don't do anything stupid," warned Chaerea.

"I have just one request," said Marcellus, causing Chaerea to roll his eyes. "I want him to still be alive when I stab him. I want him to know that it's me killing him, taking my revenge for what he did to my child."

Surprisingly, all three nodded assent. They were soldiers. They understood revenge. And they knew Marcellus was a soldier also, accustomed to killing. He would not make any mistakes. This single statement of vengeance did more to win over the three assassins than any argument Marcellus had offered before.

They waited nervously for Caligula to appear. Marcellus was the only one who was not sweating. The other three had never actually been in a battle. Marcellus had. He had learned long ago how to stifle his fear. Also, the anticipation of revenge actually excited him. He had waited a long time for this moment, and now it was here.

Finally, after a short wait which seemed like hours to them, they heard a commotion at the entrance to the tunnel. Caligula was congratulating the acting troupe of young men who had just performed for him. He turned and started walking down the tunnel. He frowned when he saw the four of them. "Chaerea, what are you doing here?" he demanded in a stern voice.

Chaerea didn't answer. He just lunged at Caligula and stabbed him in the chest. He then shouted, "Marcellus, now, if you're going to do it."

Caligula was stunned at what was happening. He made no move to try to escape. Marcellus grabbed his toga just to make sure he couldn't run away. "Now, tyrant, you will pay for what you did to my child." Caligula recognized him and was horrified at his predicament. Marcellus stabbed him rapidly three times. The others descended on the Emperor and commenced a frenzy of stabbing. Gaius Germanicus Caesar was stabbed over 30 times. He was 28 years old when he died.

He was already dead when his loyal Germanic guard showed up. They looked around but the four had already scattered. The conspirators and their new-found allies, emboldened by events, tore through the palace, looking for relatives of Caligula. They would later kill his wife and young daughter.

Meanwhile, Sylvia heard all the screaming and commotion going on outside her room. She knew she was in danger. It was only a matter of time before someone checked out her room, and perhaps mistook her for an ally or lover of Caligula. She was relieved to find the door unlocked. Even better, the guard had deserted his post.

She crept down the hall and was disconcerted to see Claudius wandering in a seeming daze. "Claudius!" she shouted. "You are in danger. You must hide."

"Who- who are you?" he stammered. He had never encountered her in the time she had been in Caligula's palace as she had been confined to her room.

"Don't you remember me, Claudius? We met years ago on the Isle of Capri. I was the lady who told you to study politics."

He considered for a moment, and then his eyes widened. "Y-yes, I do remember you. The l-lady who could t-tell the future."

"You won't have a future if you don't hide right away," she admonished. He nodded. She took his hand and led him into one of the storage rooms used by the cleaning staff. "Let's hope they don't look here," she said, as the room was only concealed by a hanging curtain.

By now, many others, who felt they had scores to settle, had joined the assassins in their killing frenzy. They eventually pushed aside the curtain in front of the storage room door where the two fugitives were hiding. They recognized Claudius immediately. Claudius closed his eyes, expecting to die in the next few seconds.

The assassins looked at each other. Chaerea shouted, "Hail Claudius Caesar Augustus, Emperor of Rome." He was hoping to avoid eventual execution by this ploy. Perhaps Claudius would feel loyalty towards him. It was a forlorn hope as Claudius did have him and his co-conspirators executed as one of his first acts.

Chapter 28

Rome 41 CE

It'd been a month since the assassination. Sylvia had finally managed to gain an audience with the new Emperor. Marcellus was still being held as a prisoner. He was the only one of the four who had not yet been executed.

"I don't know how I can allow someone who is involved in the murder of an Emperor to live." Claudius sounded adamant.

It's amazing how his stuttering has stopped, mused Sylvia incongruously. *It turns out those historians were correct, who believed Claudius was putting on an act to save himself during the reigns of Tiberius and Caligula.*

"This is different, Caesar. Marcellus is not political. His motives for killing Gaius were completely different than those of the other three. His motive was revenge for unspeakable acts of cruelty committed against us. Did you know that Gaius threw our three-year-old daughter over the cliffs at the Isle of Capri?"

Claudius looked surprised. "No, I didn't know that."

"And did you know I miscarried because of the brutal orders Gaius effected?"

"I guess I didn't know that either." Claudius hesitated, then, "He still assassinated an Emperor."

"If Gaius acted in a legal and ethical manner, then I would agree with you about what should happen to anyone who assassinated him. But we both know this is not the case. He was a brutal monster, and I'm not shy to say he deserved to die. Historians thousands of years in the future will agree with me."

Claudius became lost in thought. *Yes, this is the lady who is supposed to be able to see the future. She certainly did see my future and warned me about it.*

"There is one more thing, Caesar. Marcellus is my husband. He is a good man. I know this is not a reason to spare someone who runs afoul of the law, but I would be devastated if I lost him."

This final plea for mercy was what reached Claudius the most. *She was one of the few who treated me with kindness and respect when most others didn't. She is a good person and if she says her husband is also, I believe her.*

He stood up. "The Roman citizen Marcellus is guilty of murder. The penalty for this is death."

Sylvia teared up. "Caesar, please," she entreated.

"Allow me to finish, Madam. However, in my capacity as Emperor, I pardon him. It shall go down in the records as his being found guilty of murder and sentenced to death. The Emperor granted clemency, but it shall be recorded that he was guilty as charged."

Sylvia almost collapsed to the floor in relief. Tears streamed down her face. She sobbed, "I knew you were a good man. Your contemporary historians don't agree, but the ones from my time, will."

This disturbed Claudius a bit. "What do you mean?"

"The historians from this time, some of them a century removed from you, and possessing a certain political bias, will disparage your reign. However, historians from my time, who are much more vigilant in their research and not swayed by any kind of political bias, will report that you were one of the better emperors, perhaps in the top five of the 70 who ruled."

"Seventy emperors will rule?" Claudius was amazed.

"Yes, indeed. Of course, some of them only ruled a few months."

Marcellus and Sylvia were reunited the next day. "I am pretty sure you had something to do with my release, didn't you?"

She just smiled. "Claudius is a good man. He was one of the good emperors. He ended all the trials for treason. In some cases, he gave back the property Caligula had confiscated. He expanded the Empire a bit, the first such expansion since Augustus. And he created many public works. Perhaps the only negative in his reign is that he was the first to bribe the soldiers to support him. This dangerous precedent caused damage all through the rest of the Roman Empire. Powerful generals continued to bribe their armies to enable them to seize power.”

“Well, I was certain I was a dead man. How exactly did you convince him?”

She sighed. “It’s a long story and all my arguments were going nowhere until I appealed to his humanity and sense of justice.” She paused and then frowned. “It’s sad, really. His fourth wife, Agrippina, will poison him so that her son, Nero, can assume power.”

Marcellus grew alarmed. “Is that so? Then we must-”

“Then we must, NOTHING,” hissed Sylvia, perhaps a little too loudly. “How long have you been with me? Have you learned nothing? If this doesn’t happen 13 years from now, if he doesn’t die, history will be radically changed. For the thousandth time, I might not even exist then.”

Marcellus was chastened. “Alright, alright. I know, I know. The timeline. Stupid of me to forget.”

She grinned. “The first step to recovery is acknowledgment.”

They eventually made their way to his old wine shop. Marcipor was ecstatic to see them and his hugs were heartfelt. “Master, I would like to introduce my wife, Antonia.”

Antonia was a beauty. “What’s with this ‘master’ business, Marcipor? I already told you that when I got back, we would be partners. My only question is how someone as ugly as you could attract such a beautiful woman?”

Marcipor just laughed. “It was easy. I drugged her.”

This caused Antonia to laugh. “So that’s what happened? I often wondered.” She smiled at her husband. It was obvious to all that their marriage was a good one.

A few months passed. Their business was very prosperous and easily able to support all of them. Sylvia and Marcellus were lying in bed. "I have some news for you, Marcellus." She gave him a radiant smile. "I'm pregnant."

Chapter 29

Virginia 2021

Tegar was anxiously awaiting Sylvia's return. *Surely five minutes have already passed since she left,* he worriedly thought. This was her first time after all. She was not an experienced time traveler like Chuck. The only thing that could have prevented her returning five minutes after leaving would've been her death. And he hoped to hell that wasn't the case.

He needn't have worried, for suddenly someone appeared, seemingly out of thin air. That was the interesting thing about the quantum physics involved in time travel. Unlike most science fictions, there were no dramatic lights, or sounds, or travel through multicolored tunnels. One minute no one was there, and the next second a person appeared.

The problem was, it wasn't Sylvia who had appeared. Instead, it was a very aristocratic looking older woman. "Who-, who are you?" Tegar managed to stammer. She just smiled. Tegar approached, and looked at her more closely. "Oh my God! You are Sylvia, aren't you?" The woman looked to be at least in her 70s.

Sylvia answered in a stream of Latin, and then noticing the confusion on everyone's face, she just laughed. "Sorry, I am," she said in English. She noticed the funny looks they gave her. *I must remember. The verb, last it doesn't come. This should be spoken as 'the verb doesn't come last.'* "Old habits die hard, especially for one as old as me."

She looked around her. She had forgotten how bright everything was lit in modern times, certainly a lot brighter than the oil lamps to which she had become accustomed. And the noise. She knew she was in the basement. She knew it wouldn't be as noisy here as outside. But she was very aware of the unfamiliar humming and the occasional beep or boop. *The noise that comes from inanimate things. Not like home where people mostly make most of the noise,* she incongruously thought.

"You lived your entire life in ancient Rome, didn't you?" Tegar asked accusingly.

"Yes, Tegar. I'm sorry. Me over you, I chose. It wouldn't have made much difference anyhow, as you shall see." She said this slowly, still having a little bit of difficulty in speaking English. She still had to consciously work at not putting the verb last as was customary in Latin.

Tegar was furious, but not Chuck. He looked at her thoughtfully. *Maybe that's a choice I should've made all those years ago with Anna. Even though I'm perfectly happy with Abby and wouldn't even have met her had I made that choice.* He couldn't help admiring Sylvia's bravery.

"You do realize that your days with Tegar industries are over, as is your salary," he vehemently snapped. She just smiled. She had always been a packrat, and had more than enough money to live out her remaining years. *Too bad only five minutes have passed in this time instead of the interest I could've accrued with the over 40 years I spent in Rome. Still, with the enormous salary he was paying us, those three or four years was enough.*

"Yes, Tegar, I knew this would be the result. I hold no grudges against you. I signed the contract and knew the consequences. The only reason I returned is that I just buried my husband, Marcellus, last week, and I figured it would be much easier to spend my remaining years in a modern society with modern healthcare than in ancient Rome."

Even though she appeared to be solvent, Chuck hoped that Tegar would reconsider cutting her off, even if he had to do it on the sly, so that future time travelers wouldn't repeat the act. He resolved to talk to him about this later on, after he had cooled down.

Tegar was still seething, but he fought to control his temper. "And what of your mission? What did you find out?"

"My mission?" She was momentarily confused, but then she remembered. "Oh, the glass. I almost forgot; it was so long ago. I searched far and wide back in those early days, Tegar. I even learned the name of the man who was supposed to have created this invention." She thought for a second. "His name was Atticus something or other. I don't remember the rest, although it might come to me in the next little while. If it does, even though I no longer work for you, I shall forward this information. Anyway, Marcellus and I even found Atticus's shop. It was deserted. We searched for hours but found nothing relating to the glass."

She gave Tegar a significant look. "We think this Atticus might actually have invented the glass. We had a number of reasons for believing this. Firstly, he completely disappeared and was never seen again. The rumor was that Tiberius had him killed. Now why would he do this to an ordinary glassmaker? Secondly, we had to run for our lives from Sejanus who was Tiberius's bloodthirsty second. Somehow, he must've learned we had searched Atticus' shop. So why would he care? Unless he thought we had found the secret of the invention. Obviously, we survived Sejanus's attention. How we did is a long story which I will relate to you sometime later, if you're interested."

"So, did you finally find anything?" Tegar asked.

"Unfortunately, no. I am truly sorry, Tegar." *But I did find something, didn't I? The most marvelous man in the world who gave me the most wonderful life. Marcellus, I miss you so.*

"And what about your weapons? I don't have to tell you how dangerous this would be if they fell into the wrong hands."

"Actually, it did fall into the wrong hands when we were arrested. Fortunately, they never figured out the gun will only fire with my thumbprint. The technology was too advanced for Sejanus's people. They knew it was a weapon. The smarter ones among them like Sejanus never believed I was a goddess. Again and again, I was confronted with the truth that we had seriously underestimated the acumen of these Romans. I had been forced to use the gun a couple of times. They quickly realized a projectile had been ejected with great speed. But not having my thumb, they could not figure how this was accomplished. This almost cost me my life, by the way, until I was able to offer them something else which they found useful."

"And what was that?" Tegar asked.

"I prefer not to say. It will only piss you off." Before he could respond she returned to the subject of her gun.

 She laughed. "I cannot tell you how frustrated they were getting when they kept pressing the trigger and all they got was a click, click, click."

"And what about your electric defense, the one built into your toga?"

"They simply didn't realize there was anything special about the toga. I no longer needed it after awhile, so I quietly disposed of it."

"No chance of anyone finding it?" Tegar asked, a bit worried.

She looked at him exasperatedly. "I'm not stupid, Tegar. I burned it."

He looked at her thoughtfully. "You're the only one in the world who can answer this now, Sylvia. You realize any changes you have caused would seem normal to us, but would be apparent to you. As an example, Chuck keeps insisting I had a gorgeous executive assistant named Amanda before he left for his mission in World War II Poland. Something he did erased her existence. But I was never aware of her. As far as I was concerned, my executive assistant was Terry, and had always been Terry at that time."

He paused for a second. "Now, there are a lot of Italians today who are tall and redheaded. Did you-"

"Yes, Tegar. I had children," she interrupted. "Three girls and one boy. You know, in the beginning, I tried to avoid getting pregnant, but with a lover like Marcellus, it was an impossible task." Her expression grew saddened, "I actually had five children. My first child was a darling little girl named Livia. She was three years old when Caligula threw her over the cliffs at the Isle of Capri, in revenge for me not having allowed him to rape me."

Everyone gasped. "Marcellus almost killed him then and there. Danger to the timeline would not have stopped him. Only when I told him he could possibly be erasing my existence, did he desist."

She looked over all of them. "Gaius Germanicus Caesar, whom you know as Caligula, was a worse monster then any of your history books can tell. But Marcellus did get his revenge in the end and all without changing the timeline." *It feels so strange to be talking about things like timelines. How many years has it been?*

She looked squarely at Tegar. "I have never regretted this. Along with Marcellus, my children were the joy of my life. I did realize this would affect the timeline, but if I had to do it all over again, I would. I can't tell you how heartbreaking it was to say goodbye to them without telling where I was going, except to say they would never see me again." She teared up a bit. "My youngest daughter was very angry. She told me she would never forgive me. I almost changed my mind about leaving."

Chuck smiled at her. He couldn't blame her one bit. He decided to change the subject. "Sylvia, after all this time, did you worry that the device sending you home wouldn't work anymore?"

She turned to Chuck. He looked so young, much younger than she remembered, but then again, everyone this young looked like children to her now. "I was a bit concerned, for sure, Chuck. The battery was supposed to last over 50 years, but one can never be sure. If it killed me, I wouldn't know, would I? And to be honest, without Marcellus, I really didn't care that much. The funny thing was the trouble I had trying to remember the English words and the pattern that would send me back. It took me over an hour before I finally got it right."

"So, what do you plan on doing now?" Chuck asked.

"Well, as I told you, I have enough put away to be comfortably retired. However, I think I'll probably contact a few universities and try to correct some of their misconceptions about ancient Rome. Once my credentials are established, I'm pretty sure I'll be able to generate a little extra income this way."

"Without revealing anything about time travel," warned Tegar.

"Of course. It goes without saying. They'd probably put me in a loony bin if I did anyway," she mused.

This could be an argument I can use to convince Tegar to keep her on the payroll. Her exhaustive knowledge of ancient Rome might open up a can of worms that Tegar would prefer remain closed, Chuck thought.

She turned and looked over at all of them. "I hope you all understand, and forgive me," she said finally. She smiled at all of them, turned, and walked out the door. She missed the wink Chuck gave her.

Tegar still fumed a bit. *And now I've lost a time traveler that I spent lots of time and resources on training. I'll have to ask Chuck who is in the best position to replace her.*

They all looked at Tegar. He sighed, "Leave her be," was all he said.

ACKNOWLEDGMENTS

I can't adequately express how much I owe to my wife, the love of my life, Pam, for the creation of this manuscript. Without her help and love, I'd be lost.

I'm also grateful to my chief editor, Kim Washburn, the Word Nazi, who continues to justify her nickname with her stellar editing.

Finally, I wish to thank all of you who have read this novel and I sincerely hope you enjoyed it as much as I enjoyed writing it.